SCHOOL VERSION

Book, Music and Lyrics by

Jim Jacobs
&
Warren Casey

A SAMUEL FRENCH ACTING EDITION

SAMUEL FRENCH

FOUNDED 1830

New York Hollywood London Toronto

SAMUELFRENCH.COM

ISBN 978-0-573-60180-4   Printed in U.S.A.   #7900

IMPORTANT BILLING AND CREDIT REQUIREMENTS

All producers of **GREASE** *must* give credit to the Authors of the Work in all programs distributed in connection with performances of the Work, and in all instances in which the title of the Work appears for the purposes of advertising, publicizing or otherwise exploiting a production thereof, including, without limitation, programs, souvenir books and playbills. The names of the Authors must appear on a separate line in which no other matter appears, and *must* be in size of type not less than 50% of the size used for the title of the Work. In addition, the following *must* appear in all programs distributed in connection with performances of the play:

Billing *must* be substantially as follows:

GREASE

Book, Music and Lyrics by

Jim Jacobs and Warren Casey

Book, music and lyrics by Jim Jacobs and Warren Casey
had its premiere performance February 14, 1972
at the Eden Theatre, New York City.
It was presented by Kenneth Waissman and Maxine Fox
in association with Anthony D'Amato.

Cast
(in order of appearance)

Miss Lynch.......................................Dorothy Leon
Patty Simcox.......................................Ilene Kristen
Eugene Florczyk.......................................Tom Harris
Jan.......................................Garn Stephens
Marty.......................................Katie Hanley
Betty Rizzo.......................................Adrienne Barbeau
Doody.......................................James Canning
Roger.......................................Walter Bobbie
Kenickie.......................................Timothy Meyers
Sonny LaTierri.......................................Jim Borrelli
Frenchy.......................................Marya Small
Sandy Dumbrowski.......................................Carole Demas
Danny Zuko.......................................Barry Bostwick
Vince Fontaine.......................................Don Billett
Johnny Casino.......................................Alan Paul
Cha-Cha DiGregorio.......................................Kathi Moss
Teen Angel.......................................Alan Paul

Musical Supervision and Orchestrations by Michael Leonard
Musical Direction/Vocal and Dance Arrangements by Louis St. Louis
Scenery by Douglas W. Schmidt
Costumes by Carrie F. Robbins
Lighting by Karl Eigsti
Sound by Jack Shearing
Production Stage Manager Joe Calvan
Musical Numbers and Dances Staged by Patricia Birch

Directed by Tom Moore

Revisions to the original play
written expressly for this version by
Jim Jacobs

SYNOPSIS OF SCENES AND MUSICAL NUMBERS

ACT I

Scene 1: Reunion
"Alma Mater"   Miss Lynch, Patty and Eugene
"Alma Mater" Parody   Pink Ladies and Burger Palace Boys

Scene 2: Cafeteria and School Steps
"Summer Nights"   Sandy, Danny, Pink Ladies and
                                        Burger Palace Boys

Scene 3: School
"Those Magic Changes"   Doody, Burger Palace Boys and
                                        Pink Ladies

Scene 4: Pajama Party
"Freddy, My Love"   Marty and Pink Ladies

Scene 5: Street Corner
"Greased Lightnin'"   Kenickie and Burger Palace Boys

Scene 6: Schoolyard

Scene 7: Park
"Mooning"   Roger and Jan
"Look At Me, I'm Sandra Dee"   Rizzo
"We Go Together"   Pink Ladies and Burger Palace Boys

ACT II

Scene 1: Sandy's Bedroom and School Gym
"It's Raining on Prom Night"   Sandy and Girl's Radio Voice
"Shakin' at the High School Hop"   Johnny Casino and Company
"Born to Hand-Jive"   Johnny Casino and Company

Scene 2: In Front of the Burger Palace
"Beauty School Dropout"   Teen Angel and Chorus

Scene 3: Drive-In Movie
"Alone at a Drive-In Movie"   Danny and Burger Palace Boys

Scene 4: Jan's Party
"Rock 'n Roll Party Queen"   Doody and Roger
"Look At Me, I'm Sandra Dee"
   Reprise   Sandy

Scene 5: Inside the Burger Palace
"All Choked Up"   Sandy, Danny, Pink Ladies and
                                        Burger Palace Boys

Finale
"We Go Together" Reprise   Company

.

CHARACTERS

DANNY: The leader of the "Burger Palace Boys." Well-built, nice-looking, with an air of cool, easy-going charm. Strong and confident.

SANDY: Danny's love interest. Sweet, wholesome, naive, cute, like Sandra Dee of the "Gidget" movies.

THE PINK LADIES: The club-jacketed, gum-chewing, hip-swinging girls' gang that hangs around with the Burger Palace Boys.

RIZZO: Leader of the Pink Ladies. She is tough, sarcastic and outspoken but vulnerable. Thin, Italian, with unconventional good looks.

FRENCHY: A dreamer. Good-natured and dumb. Heavily made-up, fussy about her appearance — particularly her hair. She can't wait to finish high school so she can be a beautician.

MARTY: The "beauty" of the Pink Ladies. Pretty, looks older than the other girls, but betrays her real age when she opens her mouth. Tries to act sophisticated.

JAN: Chubby, compulsive eater. Loud and pushy with the girls, but shy with boys.

THE BURGER PALACE BOYS: A super cool, D.A.-haired, hard-looking group of high school wheeler-dealers ... or so they think.

KENICKIE: Second-in-command of the Burger Palace Boys. Tough-looking, tattooed, surly, avoids any show of softness. Has an off-beat sense of humor.

DOODY: Youngest of the guys. Small, boyish, open, with a disarming smile and a hero-worshipping attitude toward the other guys. He plays the guitar.

ROGER: The "anything-for-a-laugh" stocky type. Full of mischief, half-baked schemes and ideas. A clown who enjoys putting other people on.

SONNY: Italian-looking with shiny black hair and dark, oily skin. A braggart and wheeler-dealer who thinks he's a real lady-killer.

ADDITIONAL CHARACTERS

PATTY: A typical cheerleader at a middle-class American public high school. Attractive and atheletic. Aggressive, sure of herself, given to bursts of disconcerting enthusiasm. Catty, but in an All-American Girl sort of way. She can twirl a baton.

CHA-CHA: A blind date. Slovenly, loud-mouthed and homely. Takes pride in being "the best dancer at St. Bernadette's."

EUGENE: The class valedictorian. Physically awkward, with weak eyes and a high-pitched voice. An apple-polisher, smug and pompous but gullible.

VINCE FONTAINE: a typical "teen audience" radio disc jockey. Slick, egotistical, fast-talking. A veteran "greaser."

JOHNNY CASINO: A "greaser" student at Rydell who leads a rock 'n roll band and likes to think of himself as a real rock 'n roll idol.

TEEN ANGEL: A good-looking, falsetto-voiced Fabian-look-alike. A singer who would have caused girls to scream and riot back in 1958.

MISS LYNCH: An old maid English teacher.

ACT I

Scene 1

SCENE: Lights come up on the singing of the Rydell Alma Mater. Enter three people: MISS LYNCH, an old maid English teacher who leads the singing; PATTY, a former high school cheerleader and honor student [now a professional married career woman] and EUGENE FLORCZYK, former class valedictorian and honor student [now a vice president of an advertising agency]. There is a large sign trimmed in green and brown behind them that reads: "WELCOME BACK: RYDELL HIGH, CLASS OF '59."

ALL.
AS I GO TRAV'LING DOWN LIFE'S HIGHWAY
WHATEVER COURSE MY FORTUNES MAY FORETELL
I SHALL NOT GO ALONE ON MY WAY
FOR THOU SHALT ALWAYS BE WITH ME, RYDELL

WHEN I SEEK REST FROM WORLDLY MATTERS
IN PALACE OR IN HOVEL I MAY DWELL
AND THOUGH MY BED BE SILK OR TATTERS
MY DREAMS SHALL ALWAYS BE OF THEE, RYDELL

(EUGENE, PATTY and MISS LYNCH enter.)

THROUGH ALL THE YEARS, RYDELL
AND TEARS, RYDELL
WE GIVE THREE CHEERS, RYDELL, FOR THEE
THROUGH EV'RYTHING, RYDELL
WE CLING, RYDELL
AND SING, RYDELL, TO THEE

(As the songs ends, MISS LYNCH introduces EUGENE and then takes her seat.)

9

MISS LYNCH. Thank you. It is my pleasure at this time to introduce Mrs. Patricia Simcox Honeywell, your class yearbook editor, and Mr. Eugene Florczyk, class valedictorian and today vice president of "Straight-Shooters" Unlimited, Research and Marketing.

EUGENE. Miss Lynch, fellow graduates, honored guests, and others. Looking over these familiar faces really takes me back to those wonderful bygone days. Days of working and playing together, days of cheering together for our athletic teams—Yay, Ringtails!—and days of worrying together when examination time rolled around. Perhaps some of those familiar faces of yesteryear are absent this evening because they thought our beloved Miss Lynch might have one of her famous English finals awaiting us. *(To MISS LYNCH.)* I was only joking. *(To audience.)* However, the small portion of alumni I notice missing tonight are certainly not missing from our fond memories of them ... and I'm sure they'd want us to know that they're fully present and accounted for in spirit, just the way we always remember them.

(School bell rings—"Chuck Berry" guitar run is heard. The GREASERS are revealed in positions of laziness, defiance, boredom and amusement. They sing a parody of the Alma Mater as they take over the stage.)

GREASERS.
I SAW A DEAD SKUNK ON THE HIGHWAY
AND I WAS GOING CRAZY FROM THE SMELL
'CAUSE WHEN THE WIND WAS BLOWIN' MY WAY
IT SMELLED JUST LIKE THE HALLS OF OLD RYDELL
AND IF YOU GOTTA USE THE LUNCH ROOM
AND LATER ON YOU START TO PUKE AND SMELL
WELL YOU HAD BETTER SEE A DOCTOR
'CAUSE YOU GOT MEMORIES OF OLD RYDELL

I CAN'T EXPLAIN, RYDELL, THIS PAIN, RYDELL
IS IT PTOMAINE, RYDELL, GAVE ME?
IS IT T.B. RYDELL? COULD BE RYDELL.
YOU OUGHTTA SEE THE FACULTY

IF MR. CLEAN, RYDELL, HAD SEEN RYDELL
HE'D JUST TURN GREEN AND DISAPPEAR
I'M OUTTA LUCK, RYDELL
DEAD DUCK, RYDELL
I'M STUCK, RYDELL, RIGHT HERE!!!!!!

Scene 2

SCENE: The GREASERS stalk off as the scene shifts to the high school cafeteria. JAN and MARTY enter wearing their Pink Ladies jackets and carrying trays, JAN's loaded with food. As each female character enters, she joins the others at one large table.

JAN. Jeez, I wish it was still summer. Look, it's only a quarter after twelve and I feel like I've been here a whole year already.

MARTY. Yeah, what a drag. Hey, you wanna sit here?

JAN. Yeah, Rizzo's coming and Frenchy's bringing that new chick.

MARTY. Huh. You want my coleslaw?

(JAN grabs it.)

JAN. I'll see if I have room for it.

(RIZZO enters.)

MARTY. Hey, Rizzo, over here! (handshake?)

RIZZO. Hey, Hey, Hey! Where's all the guys?

JAN. Those slobs. You think they'd spend a dime on their lunch? They're baggin' it.

RIZZO. Pretty cheap. (end up down stage front)

(Lights fade on the cafeteria, come up on ROGER and DOODY sitting on the school steps.)

DOODY Hey, Rump, I'll trade you a sardine for a peanut butter and jelly.

ROGER. I ain't eating one of those things. You had 'em in your ice box since last Easter.

(KENICKIE enters.)

KENICKIE. Hey! Where you at?

ROGER. Hey, Kenickie. What's happening?

DOODY. Hey, Kenickie!

ROGER. Hey, Knicks, where were ya all summer?

KENICKIE. Luggin' boxes at Bargain City

DOODY. WOOOO!

ROGER. Nice Job!

KENICKIE. Hey, cram it! I'm saving up to get me some wheels.

ROGER. You gettin' a car, Kenicks?

DOODY. Hey, cool! What kind?

KENICKIE. I don't know what kind yet, moron. But I got a name all picked out: "Greased Lightnin!"

ROGER. Oh, nifty!

(ROGER does pig snorts, DOODY laughs, SONNY enters wearing wraparound sunglasses. As he enters, he pulls a class schedule out of his pocket.)

KENICKIE. Hey, whattaya say, Sonny?

SONNY. Drop dead! I got Old Lady Lynch for English again. She hates my guts.

ROGER. Nah, she thinks you're cute, Sonny. *(GUYS laugh.)* That's why she keeps puttin' ya back in her class.

SONNY. Yeah, well, this year she's gonna wish she never seen me.

KENICKIE. Oh, Yeah?!

SONNY. I'm just not gonna take any of her lip, that's all. I don't take that jive from nobody.

(MISS LYNCH enters.)

MISS LYNCH. What's all the racket out here?

DOODY. Hi, Miss Lynch.

ROGER. Hello, Miss Lynch.

MISS LYNCH. Dominic, aren't you supposed to be in class right now?

SONNY. Yes, Ma'am.

DOODY and ROGER. Yes, Ma'am.

MISS LYNCH. That's a fine way to start the new semester, Mr. LaTierri.

DOODY and ROGER. Mr. LaTierri.

MISS LYNCH. Well? Are you going to stand there all day?

SONNY. No, Ma'am.

DOODY and ROGER. No, Ma'am.

MISS LYNCH. Then move!

(LYNCH exits)

SONNY. Yes, Ma'am.
DOODY and ROGER. Yes, Ma'am.
ROGER. I'm sure glad she didn't give you any "lip," Son. You would have really told her off, right?
SONNY. Shaddup!

(Lights fade on steps, come up again on GIRLS in cafeteria.)

MARTY. Hey, Jan, who's that chick with Frenchy? Is she the one you were tellin' me about?
JAN. Yeah, her name's Sandy. She seems pretty cool. Maybe we could let her in the Pink Ladies.
RIZZO. Just what we need. Another chick hangin' around.

(FRENCHY and SANDY enter, carrying trays.)

FRENCHY. Hi, you guys. This is my new next-door neighbor, Sandy Dumbrowski. This here's Rizzo and that's Marty and you remember Jan.
JAN. Sure, hi.
SANDY. Hi. Pleased to meet you.
FRENCHY. Come on, sit down.
RIZZO. How long you been livin' around here?
SANDY. Since July. My father just got transferred here.
JAN. You gonna eat your coleslaw, Sandy?
SANDY. It smells kinda funny.
FRENCHY. Wait'll you have the chipped beef. Better known as "Barf on a Bun."
JAN. How do you like the school so far, Sandy?
SANDY. Oh, it seems real nice. I was going to go to Immaculata, but my father had a fight with the Mother Superior over my patent leather shoes.
JAN. What do ya' mean?
SANDY. She said boys could see up my dress in the reflection.
MARTY. Swear to God?
JAN. Hey, where do ya get shoes like that?
PATTY. *(Offstage.)* Hi kids!!!!!!!!!!!!!!!

RIZZO. Look who's comin. Patty Simcox, the little Lulu of Rydell High.

ALL. Oh no!!!!!!!!!!!!! There is a fungus among-gus.

(PATTY enters in cheerleader outfit.)

PATTY. Well, don't say hello.

RIZZO. We won't.

PATTY. Is there room at your table?

MARTY. Oh, yeah, move over, French.

PATTY. Oh, I just love the first day of school, don't you?

RIZZO. It's the biggest thrill of my life.

(FRENCHY starts doing RIZZO's hair.)

PATTY. You'll never guess what happened this morning

RIZZO. Prob'ly not.

PATTY. Well, they announced this year's nominees for the student council, and guess who's up for Vice President?

MARTY. *(Knowing what's coming.)* Who?

PATTY. Me! Isn't that wild?

RIZZO. Wild.

PATTY. Oh, you must think I'm a terrible clod! I never even bothered to introduce myself to your new friend.

SANDY. Oh, I'm Sandy Dumbrowski.

PATTY. It's a real pleasure, Sandy. We certainly are glad to have you here at Rydell.

SANDY. Thanks.

MARTY. Aaaaaaaahhh, shoo-oot!

PATTY. Goodness gracious.

RIZZO. Oooo. Naughty-naughty. What was that all about?

MARTY. *(Examining her glasses.)* One of my diamonds fell in the macaroni.

(Lights fade on GIRLS, come up on GUYS on the steps.)

DOODY. Hey, ain't that Danny over there?

SONNY. Where?

DOODY. HEY, DANNY! WHATCHA DOIN?

ROGER. That's good, Dood. Play it real cool.

DANNY. *(Crossing to GUYS, carrying books and lunch bag.)*

Hey, you guys, what's shakin'?

DOODY. Where ya been all summer, Danny?

DANNY. Well, I spent a lot of time down at the beach.

KENICKIE. Hey, didja meet any new chicks?

DANNY. Nah.

ALL. Come on, Zuko .... *(Adlibs.)*

DANNY. Just met this one that was sorta cool, ya know?

ALL. Oh, yeah. *(Adlib nods and giggles.)*

DANNY. You don't want to hear all the mushy details, anyway.

SONNY and GUYS. Sure we do! Let's hear a little!

(Miscellaneous adlibs. GUYS join in playfully mauling DANNY as the lights fade on them and come back up on the GIRLS at the cafeteria table.)

SANDY. I spent most of the summer down at the beach.

JAN. What for? We got a brand new pool right in the neighborhood. It's real nice.

RIZZO. Yeah, if you like swimmin' in Clorox.

SANDY. Well — — actually, I met a boy there.

MARTY. You hauled your cookies all the way to the beach for some guy?

SANDY. This was sort of a special boy.

RIZZO. Are you kiddin'? There ain't no such thing.

(Lights stay up on GIRLS, come up on GUYS.)

Song: "SUMMER NIGHTS"

DANNY.
SUMMER LOVIN'! HAD ME A BLAST
    SANDY.
SUMMER LOVIN'! HAPPENED SO FAST
    DANNY.
MET A GIRL CRAZY FOR ME
    SANDY.
MET A BOY CUTE AS CAN BE
    BOTH.
SUMMER DAY, DRIFTING AWAY, TO
UH-OH, THOSE SUMMER NIGHTS.

GUYS.
TELL ME MORE, TELL ME MORE,
C'MON LET'S HEAR THE DIRT!
GIRLS.
TELL ME MORE, TELL ME MORE
MARTY.
DOES HE DRIVE A CONVERT?
DANNY.
TOOK HER BOWLING, IN THE ARCADE
SANDY.
WE WENT STROLLING, DRANK LEMONADE
DANNY.
WE TOLD JOKES UNDER THE DOCK
SANDY.
WE STAYED OUT TILL TEN O'CLOCK
BOTH.
SUMMER FLING, DON'T MEAN A THING,
BUT UH-OH THOSE SUMMER NIGHTS
GUYS.
TELL ME MORE, TELL ME MORE,
BUT YA DON'T HAVE TO BRAG
GIRLS.
TELL ME MORE, TELL ME MORE
RIZZO.
'CAUSE HE SOUNDS LIKE A DRAG
SANDY.
HE GOT FRIENDLY, HOLDING MY HAND
DANNY.
SHE GOT FRIENDLY, OUT ON THE SAND
SANDY.
HE WAS SWEET, JUST TURNED EIGHTEEN
DANNY.
SHE WAS SHARP, LIKE YOU'VE NEVER SEEN
BOTH.
SUMMER HEAT, BOY AND GIRL MEET,
THEN UH-OH, THOSE SUMMER NIGHTS!
GIRLS.
TELL ME MORE, TELL ME MORE
JAN.
HOW MUCH DOUGH DID HE SPEND?

GUYS.
TELL ME MORE, TELL ME MORE
    SONNY.
COULD SHE GET ME A FRIEND?
    SANDY.
IT TURNED COLDER, THAT'S WHERE IT ENDS
    DANNY.
SO I TOLD HER WE'D STILL BE FRIENDS
    SANDY.
THEN WE MADE OUR TRUE LOVE VOW
    DANNY.
WONDER WHAT SHE'S DOING NOW?
    BOTH.
SUMMER DREAMS, RIPPED AT THE SEAMS,
BUT, UH-OOH! THOSE SUMMER NIGHTS!
    GIRLS and GUYS.
TELL ME MORE, TELL ME MORE - OR- ORE!!!!!!!!!!!

(Lights stay up on both groups after song.)

    PATTY. Gee, he sounds wonderful, Sandy.
    DOODY. She really sounds cool, Danny.
    RIZZO. This guy sounds like a drip.
    KENICKIE. She Catholic?
    JAN. What if we said that about Danny Zuko?
    SONNY. Hot stuff, huh, Zuker?
    SANDY. Did you say Danny Zuko?
    DANNY. I didn't say that, Sonny!
    RIZZO. Hey, was he the guy?
    DOODY. Boy, you get all the "neats!"
    SANDY. Doesn't he go to Lake Forest Academy?
    KENICKIE. She doesn't go to Rydell, does she?
    MARTY. That's a laugh!
    SONNY. Too bad, I bet she'd go for me.
    PATTY. Listen, Sandy, forget Danny Zuko. I know some really
nice boys.
    RIZZO. So do I. Right, you guys? C'mon let's go.

(PINK LADIES get up from the table, SANDY following them. The

GUYS *all laugh together.)*

FRENCHY. See ya 'round Patty!

RIZZO. Yeah, maybe we'll drop in on the next Student Council meeting.

(RIZZO nudges MARTY in the ribs.
Lights go down on the lunchroom, GIRLS cross toward GUYS on steps.)

MARTY. Well, speaking of the devil!

SONNY. What'd I tell ya, they're always chasin' me.

MARTY. Not you, greaseball! Danny!

RIZZO. Yeah. We got a surprise for ya.

(PINK LADIES shove SANDY toward DANNY.)

SANDY. *(Nervous.)* Hello, Danny!

DANNY. *(Uptight.)* Oh, hi. How are ya?

SANDY. Fine.

DANNY. Oh yeah ... I .... ugh ... thought you were goin' to Immaculata.

SANDY. I changed my plans.

DANNY. Yeah! Well, that's cool. I'll see ya around. Let's go you guys!

(He pushes GUYS out.)

JAN. *(Picking up DANNY's brown paper lunch bag.)* Gee, he was so glad to see ya, he dropped his lunch.

SANDY. I don't get it. He was so nice this summer.

FRENCHY. Don't worry about it, Sandy.

MARTY. Hey listen, how'd you like to come over to my house tonight? It'll be just us girls.

JAN. Yeah, those guys are all a bunch of creeps.

(DANNY returns for his lunch. JAN is eating his apple.)

RIZZO. Yeah, Zuko's the biggest creep of all!

(RIZZO, seeing DANNY, exits. Other GIRLS follow pulling SANDY off with them.)

Scene 3

SCENE: School bell rings and class change begins. GREASERS, PATTY and EUGENE enter, go to lockers, get books, etc. DANNY sees DOODY with guitar.

DANNY. Hey, Doody, where'dja get the guitar?

DOODY. I just started takin' lessons this summer.

DANNY. Can you play anything on it?

DOODY. Sure. *(He fumbles with the frets and strikes a sour chord.)* That's a "C."

(DOODY sits and waits for approval.)

MARTY. Hey, that's pretty good.

DOODY. *(Hitting each chord badly.)* Then I know an A Minor, and an F, and I've been working on a G.

FRENCHY. Hey! Can you play "Tell Laura I Love Her"?

DOODY. I don't know. Has it got a "C" in it?

DANNY. Hey, come on. Let's hear a little, Elvis.

DOODY. *(Pulling out instruction book.)* … "Magic Changes" by Ronny Dell……………… *(He sings off-key.)*

C-C-C-C-C-C

A-A-A-A MINOR

F-F-F-F-F-F

G-G-G-G SEVEN

DANNY. That's terrific.

DOODY. Thanks—want to hear it again?

ALL. Sure! Yeah! *(Etc.…)*

(DOODY starts to sing and other KIDS transform into rock 'n roll, 'doo-wop' group backing him as he suddenly becomes a teen idol rock 'n roll star.)

Song: *"THOSE MAGIC CHANGES"*

DOODY and GROUP.

C-C-C-C-C-C

A-A-A-A MINOR

F-F-F-F-F-F
G-G-G-G SEVENTH

WHAT'S THAT PLAYING ON THE RADIO?
WHY DO I START SWAYING TO AND FRO?
I HAVE NEVER HEARD THAT SONG BEFORE
BUT IF I DON'T HEAR IT ANY MORE
IT'S STILL FAMILIAR TO ME
SENDS A THRILL RIGHT THROUGH ME
'CAUSE THOSE CHORDS REMIND ME OF
THE NIGHT THAT I FIRST FELL IN LOVE TO
THOSE MAGIC CHANGES.

MY HEART ARRANGES A MELODY
THAT'S NEVER THE SAME
A MELODY
THAT'S CALLING YOUR NAME
AND BEGS YOU, PLEASE, COME BACK TO ME
PLEASE RETURN TO ME
DON'T GO AWAY AGAIN
OH, MAKE THEM PLAY AGAIN
THE MUSIC I LONG TO HEAR
AS ONCE AGAIN YOU WHISPER IN MY EAR

I'LL BE WAITING BY THE RADIO
YOU'LL COME BACK TO ME SOME DAY I KNOW
BEEN SO LONESOME SINCE YOUR LAST GOODBYE
BUT I'M SINGING AS I CRY-Y-Y
WHILE THE BASS IS SOUNDING
WHILE THE DRUMS ARE POUNDING
BEATING OF MY BROKEN HEART
WILL CLIMB TO FIRST PLACE ON THE CHART
OHHH, MY HEART ARRANGES
OHHH, THOSE MAGIC CHANGES

C-C-C-C-C-C
A-A-A-A MINOR
F-F-F-F-F-F
G-G-G-G SEVENTH
SHOOP DOO WAH!

*(At the end of the song, MISS LYNCH enters to break up the group.
ALL exit, except GUYS and SONNY.)*

MISS LYNCH. *(To SONNY.)* Mr. LaTierri, aren't you due in
Detention Hall right now?

(GUYS all make fun of SONNY and lead him off to Detention Hall.)

Scene 4

*SCENE: A pajama party in MARTY's bedroom. MARTY, FRENCHY,
JAN and RIZZO are in pastel baby doll pajamas, SANDY in a
quilted robe buttoned all the way up to the neck. The WAXX
jingle for the VINCE FONTAINE show is playing on the radio.*

VINCE'S RADIO VOICE. Hey, hey, this is the main-brain,
Vince Fontaine, at Big Fifteen! Spinnin' the stacks of wax, here at the
House of Wax—W-A-X-X *(OOO-ga horn sound.)* Cruisin' time,
10:46. *(Sound of ricocheting bullet.)* Sharpshooter pick hit of the
week. A brand new one shootin' up the charts like a rocket by "The
Vel-doo Rays"—goin' out to Ronnie and Sheila, the kids down at
Mom's school store, and especially to Little Joe and the LaDons—
listen in while I give it a spin!

*(Radio fades. FRENCHY is looking at a fan magazine that has a big
picture of Fabian.)* (sitting on bed)

JAN. Hey, Sandy, you ever wear earrings? I think they'd keep
your face from lookin' so skinny.
    MARTY. Hey! Yeah! I got some big round ones made out of real
mink. They'd look great on you.
    FRENCHY. Wouldja like me to pierce your ears for ya, Sandy?
I'm gonna be a beautician, y'know.   S: aint it dangeras
    JAN. Yeah, she's real good. She did mine for me.   R: what? you
    FRENCHY. Hey, Marty, you got a needle around?   arent afraid
    MARTY. Hey, how about my circle pin?   are ya?
    SANDY. Uh ... maybe ... uh ....   S: of course not

(MARTY reaches for her Pink Ladies jacket, takes off "circle pin"

and hands it to FRENCHY.)

FRENCHY. Hey, would ya hold still!

(FRENCHY begins to pierce SANDY's ears. SANDY yelps.)

MARTY. Hey, French ... why don't you take Sandy in the john? My old lady'd kill me if we got blood all over the rug.
SANDY. Huh?
FRENCHY. It only bleeds for a second. Come on.
JAN. Aaawww! We miss all the fun!
SANDY. Listen, I'm sorry, but I'm not feeling too well, and I ....
RIZZO. Look, Sandy, if you think you're gonna be hangin' around with the Pink Ladies — you gotta get with it! Otherwise, forget it ... and go back to your hot cocoa and Girl Scout cookies!
SANDY. Okay, come on .... Frenchy.

(SANDY exits slowly.)

JAN. Hey, Sandy, don't sweat it. If she screws up, she can always fix your hair so your ears won't show.
FRENCHY. Har-dee-har-har!

(FRENCY exits.)

RIZZO. That chick's getting to be a real pain.
JAN. Ah, lay off, Rizzo
SANDY. *(Offstage.)* Urghhhhhhhhhhhhhhhh!!!!!
RIZZO. What was that?
FRENCHY. *(Running back into room.)* Hey, Marty, Sandy's sick. She's heavin' all over the place.
JAN. Ja do her ears already?
FRENCHY. Nah. I only did one. As soon as she saw the blood she went BLEUGH!!!!!!!!!!!!
MARTY. *(Making a big show of putting on a gaudy kimono.)* Jeez, it's getting kinda chilly. I think I'll put my robe on.
JAN. Hey, Marty. Wher'dja get that thing?
MARTY. Oh, you like it? It's from Japan. This guy I know sent it to me.
FRENCHY. No kiddin'!

MARTY. He's a Marine. And, a real doll too!

FRENCHY. Oh, wow! Hey, Marty, can he get me one of those things?

JAN. You never told us you knew any Marines.

RIZZO. How long you known this guy?

MARTY. Oh .... just a couple of months. I met him on a blind date at the roller rink ... and the next thing I know, he joins up. Anyway, right off the bat he starts sendin' me things and then today I get this kimono. Oh yeah, and look what else!

(MARTY pulls out ring.)

ALL. AHHHHHHHHH!!!!!!!!!!!!!!

FRENCHY. Jeez! Engaged to a Marine!

RIZZO. Endsville.

JAN. What's this guy look like, Marty?

FRENCHY. Ya got a picture?

MARTY. Yeah, but it's not too good. He ain't in uniform. *(MARTY takes her wallet out of the dresser. It's one of those fat bulging ones with rubber bands around it. She swings wallet and accordion picture folder drops to floor.)* Oh, here it is ... next to Paul Anka.

JAN. How come it's ripped in half?

MARTY. Oh, his old girlfriend was in the picture.

JAN. What's this guy's name anyway?

MARTY. Oh! It's Freddy. Freddy Strulka.

JAN. Strulka. Is that Polish?

MARTY. Naah. I think he's Irish.

FRENCHY. Do you write him a lot, Marty?

MARTY. Pretty much. Every time I get a present.

JAN. Whattaya say to a guy in a letter, anyway?

Song: "FREDDY MY LOVE"

MARTY.
FREDDY, MY LOVE, I MISS YOU MORE THAN WORDS CAN
     SAY
FREDDY, MY LOVE, PLEASE KEEP IN TOUCH WHILE YOU'RE
     AWAY
HEARING FROM YOU CAN MAKE THE DAY SO MUCH BETTER

GETTING A SOUVENIR OR MAYBE A LETTER
I REALLY FLIPPED OVER THE GREY CASHMERÉ SWEATER
FREDDY MY LOVE, FREDDY MY LOVE, FREDDY MY LOVE,
 FREDDY MY LOVE.

DON'T KEEP YOUR LETTERS FROM ME
I THRILL TO EVERY LINE
YOUR SPELLING'S KINDA CRUMMY
BUT HONEY, SO IS MINE
I TREASURE EVERY GIFTIE
THE RING IS REALLY NIFTIE
YOU SAY IT COST YOU FIFTY
SO YOU'RE THRIFTY
I DON'T MIND

FREDDY YOU'LL SEE, YOU'LL HAVE ME IN YOUR ARMS
 SOMEDAY
AND I'LL BE HOLDING MY BRIDAL BOUQUET
THINKING ABOUT IT, MY HEARTS POUNDING ALREADY
KNOWING WHEN YOU COME HOME WE'LL START GOING
 STEADY
AND THROW YOUR SERVICE PAY AROUND LIKE CONFETTI

FREDDY MY LOVE,
FREDDY MY LOVE, FREDDY MY LOVE, FREDDY MY LOVE,
FREDDY MY LOVE, FREDDY MY LOVE, FREDDY MY LOVE,
OOH, OOH, OOH, OOH!!!!!!!!!!!!
FREDDY MY LOOOOOOOVE!!!!!!!

 RIZZO.
FREDDY MY LOVE, FREDDY MY LOVE, FREDDY MY LOVE

(On the last few bars of song the GIRLS fall asleep one by one, until
 RIZZO is the only one left awake. She pulls pants on over her
 pajamas and climbs out the window. Just at that moment, SANDY
 comes back into the room unnoticed by RIZZO. SANDY stands
 looking after her.)

Scene 5

SCENE: Guys come running on out of breath, and carrying flashlights and four hubcaps. DANNY has a tire iron.

DANNY. I don't know why I brought this tire iron! I coulda yanked these babies off with my bare hands!

SONNY. Sure ya could, Zuko! I just broke six fingernails!

ROGER. Hey, what idiot would put brand new hubcaps on some old, beat-up jalopy?!

DANNY. Probably some real tool!

(A car horn is heard.)

SONNY. Hey, here comes that car we just hit! Ditch the evidence!

(GUYS run, dropping hubcaps. SONNY tries to scoop them up as KENICKIE drives on in "Greased Lightning.")

KENICKIE. All right, put those things back on the car, dipstick!

DANNY. Hey, it's Kenickie!

SONNY. Jeez, whatta grouch! We was only holdin' 'em for ya so nobody'd swipe 'em.

DANNY. Kenickie, whattaya doin' with this hunk-ah-junk, anyway?

KENICKIE. Whattaya mean? This is "Greased Lightning."

(All the GUYS jaws drop.)

ROGER. What? You really expect to pick up chicks in this sardine can?

KENICKIE. *(Shakes fist.)* Hey, right here, Rump! Wait till I give it a paint job and soup up the engine—she'll work like a champ.

DANNY. Ladies and gentlemen, the one and only "Greased Lightning!"

Song: "GREASED LIGHTNIN"

KENICKIE.
I'LL HAVE ME OVERHEAD LIFTERS AND FOUR-BARREL

QUADS, OH, YEAH
A FUEL INJECTION CUT-OFF AND CHROME-PLATED RODS,
    OH, YEAH
WITH A FOUR-SPEED ON THE FLOOR THEY'LL BE WAITIN'
    AT THE DOOR
YA KNOW WITHOUT A DOUBT, I'M GONNA PEEL OUT
IN GREASED LIGHTNIN'

KENICKIE and GUYS.
GO, GREASED LIGHTNIN', YOU'RE BURNING UP THE
    QUARTER MILE
            (GREASED LIGHTNIN', GO GREASED LIGHTNIN')
GO, GREASED LIGHTNIN', YOU'RE COASTIN' THROUGH THE
    HEAT-LAP TRIALS
            (GREASED LIGHTNIN', GO GREASED LIGHTNIN')
YOU ARE SUPREME
THE CHICKS'LL SCREAM
FOR GREASED LIGHTNIN'

KENICKIE.
I'LL HAVE ME PURPLE FRENCHED TAIL-LIGHTS AND
    THIRTY-INCH FINS, OH YEAH
A PALOMINO DASHBOARD AND DUAL MUFFLER TWINS,
    OH YEAH
WITH NEW PISTONS, PLUGS, AND SHOCKS, SHE CAN BEAT
    THE SUPER-STOCKS
YA KNOW THAT I AIN'T BRAGGIN', SHE'S A REAL DRAGGIN'
    WAGON.
GREASED LIGHTNIN'!

KENICKIE and GUYS.
GO, GREASED LIGHTNIN', YOU'RE BURNIN' UP THE
    QUARTER MILE
            (GREASED LIGHTNIN', GO, GREASED LIGHTNIN')
YEAH, GREASED LIGHTNIN', YOU'RE COASTIN' THROUGH
    THE HEAT-LAP TRIALS
            (GREASED LIGHTNIN', YEAH, GREASED LIGHTNIN')
YOU ARE SUPREME
THE CHICKS'LL SCREAM
FOR GREASED LIGHTNIN'!

(As song ends, RIZZO enters.) right*

RIZZO. What the heck is that ugly lookin' thing?!

KENICKIE. This is "Greased Lightnin!" Ain't it cool?

RIZZO. Yeah. About as cool as a garbage truck. Out! *(RIZZO opens the passenger door, shoving GUYS out.)* Hey Danny, I just left your girlfriend over at Marty's house, heavin' all over the place.

DANNY. Whattaya' talkin' about?

RIZZO. Sandy Dumbrowski! Y'know .... Sandra Dee. HA!

KENICKIE. Be cool, you guys.

DANNY. Hey, you better tell that to Rizzo!

(Sirens sound.)

KENICKIE. The Fuzz! You guys better get ridda those hubcaps!

DANNY. Whattaya mean, man? They're yours!

(GUYS throw hubcaps on car hood.)

KENICKIE. Oh no, they're not. I stole 'em.

(KENICKIE starts to drive off. Siren sounds again. All GUYS leap on car, drive off, singing: "Go Greased Lightning" etc., as the lights change to new scene.)

Scene 6

SCENE: SANDY runs on with pom poms, dressed in a green baggy gym suit. She does a Rydell cheer.

SANDY.
DO A SPLIT, GIVE A YELL
THROW A FIT FOR OLD RYDELL
WAY TO GO, GREEN AND BROWN
TURN THE FOE UPSIDE DOWN

(SANDY does awkward split. DANNY enters.)

DANNY. Hiya, Sandy. *(SANDY gives him a startled look.)* Hey, what happened to your ear?

SANDY. *(She turns her head downstage so that the audience sees the big white Band-Aid on her ear.)* Huh? *(She covers her ear with her hand, answers coldly.)* Oh, nothing. Just an accident.

DANNY. Hey, look, uh, I hope you're not bugged about that first day at school. I mean, couldn't ya tell I was glad to see ya?

SANDY. Well, you've could've been a little nicer to me in front of your friends.

DANNY. Are you kiddin'!? You don't know those guys! I mean.... *(Awkward pause)* Listen, if it was up to me. I'd never even look at any other chick but you. Hey, tell ya what. We're throwin' a party in the park tomorrow night for Frenchy. She's gonna quit school before she flunks again and go to beauty school. How'dja like to make it on down there with me?

SANDY. I'd really like to, but I'm not so sure those girls want me around anymore.

DANNY. Listen, Sandy. Nobody's gonna start gettin' salty with ya when I'm around. Uh-uhh!

SANDY. All right, Danny, as long as you're with me. Let's not let anyone come between us again, okay?

PATTY. *(Rushing onstage with two batons and wearing cheerleader outfit.)* HIIIIIiiiii, DANNY! Oh, don't let me interrupt. *(Gives SANDY baton.)* Here, why don't you twirl this for awhile. *(Taking DANNY aside.)* I've been dying to tell you something. You know what I found out after you left my house the other night? My mother thinks you're cute. *(To SANDY.)* He's such a lady-killer.

SANDY. Isn't he though! What were you doing at her house?

DANNY. Ah, I was just copying down some homework.

PATTY. Come on, Sandy, let's practice.

SANDY. Yeah, let's! I'm just dying to make a good impression on all those cute lettermen.

DANNY. Oh, that's why you're wearing that thing—gettin' ready to show off in front of a bunch of lame-brain jocks?

SANDY. Don't tell me you're jealous, Danny.

DANNY. What? Of that bunch ah meatheads! Don't make me laugh. Ha! Ha!

SANDY. Just because they can do something you can't do?

DANNY. Yeah, sure, right.

SANDY. Okay, what have *you* ever done?

DANNY. *(To PATTY twirling baton.)* Stop that! I won a Hully-

Gully contest at the "Teen Talent" record hop.

SANDY. Aahhh, you don't even know what I'm talking about.

DANNY. Whattaya mean, look, I could run circles around those jerks.

SANDY. But you'd rather spend your time copying other people's homework.

DANNY. Listen, the next time they have tryouts for any of those teams I'll show you what I can do.

PATTY. Oh, what a lucky coincidence! The track team's having tryouts tomorrow.

DANNY. *(Panic.)* Huh? Okay, I'll be there.

SANDY. Big talk.

DANNY. You think so, huh. Hey, Patty, when'dja say those tryouts were?

PATTY. Tomorrow, tenth period on the football field.

DANNY. Good, I'll be there. You're gonna come watch me, aren't you?

PATTY. Oh, I can't wait!

DANNY. Solid. I'll see ya there, baby doll.

(DANNY exits.)

PATTY. Toodles! Ooohh, I'm so excited, aren't you?

SANDY. Come on, let's practice!!!!!!

(Twirling batons, SANDY just missing PATTY'S head with each swing.)

SANDY, PATTY and CHEERLEADERS.
HIT 'EM AGAIN, RYDELL RINGTAILS
TEAR 'EM APART, GREEN AND BROWN
BASH THEIR BRAINS OUT, STOMP 'EM ON THE FLOOR
FOR THE GLORY OF RYDELL EVER MORE.

FIGHT TEAM, FIGHT, FIGHT, TEAM FIGHT
CHEW 'EM UP — SPIT 'EM OUT
FIGHT TEAM, FIGHT

(SANDY and PATTY exit doing majorette march step.)

Scene 7

SCENE: A deserted section of the park. JAN and ROGER on picnic table. RIZZO and KENICKIE on bench. MARTY sitting on other bench. FRENCHY and SONNY on blanket reading fan magazines. DANNY pacing. DOODY sitting on a trash can. A portable radio is playing "The Vince Fontaine Show."

VINCE'S RADIO VOICE. Hey, gettin' back on the rebound here for our second half. *(Cuckoo sound.)* Dancin' Word Bird Contest comin' up in a half hour, when maybe I'll call you. Hey, I think you'll like this little ditty from the city, a new group discovered by Alan Freed. Turn up the sound and stomp on the ground. Ohhh, yeah!!!

(Radio fades.)

DANNY. Hey, French, when do ya start beauty school?

FRENCHY. Next week. I can hardly wait. No more dumb books and boring teachers.

DOODY. Hey, Rump. You shouldn't be eatin' that cheeseburger. It's still Friday, y'know!

ROGER. Ah, for cryin' out loud. What'dja remind me for? Now I gotta go to confession.

JAN. Well, I can eat anything. That's the nice thing about bein' a Lutheran.

ROGER. Yeah, that's the nice thing about bein' Petunia Pig.

JAN. Drop dead!

FRENCHY. Hey, Sonny, don't maul that magazine. There's a picture of Ricky Nelson in there I really wanna save.

SONNY. Yeah. Yeah, like Ricky Nelson really knows you exist.

(FRENCHY sticks her tongue out at SONNY.)

MARTY. Hey, Danny, how do I look as a college girl?

DANNY. *(Pulling her letterman sweater.)* Boola-Boola

MARTY. Hey, watch it! It belongs to this big jock at Holy Contrition.

DANNY. Oh, yeah. Wait'll ya see me wearin' one of those things. I tried out for the track team today.

MARTY. Are you serious? With those bird legs?

(KIDS all laugh. ROGER does funny imitation of DANNY as a gung-ho track star.)

ROGER. WHUP, WHUP, WHUP.... WOAH WHUP, WHUP, WHUP.... WAOH.

DANNY. Hey, better hobby than yours. Rump.

ALL. Rump, Rump, Rump, Rump.

JAN. How come you never get mad at those guys?

ROGER. Why should I?

JAN. Well, that name they call you. Rump!

GUYS. Rump, Rump, Rump, Rump.

ROGER. That's just my nickname. It's sorta like a title.

GUYS. Rump, Rump, Rump, Rump.

JAN. Whattaya mean?

ROGER. I'm king of the mooners.

JAN. The what?

ROGER. I'm the mooning champ of Rydell High

JAN. You mean showin' off your bare behind to people? That's pretty raunchy.

ROGER. Nah, it's neat! I even mooned Old Lady Lynch once. I hung one on her right out the car window. And she never even knew who it was.

JAN. Too much! I wish I'd been there. I mean ... y'know what I mean.

ROGER. Yeah, I wish you'd been there too.

JAN. You do?

Song: *"MOONING"*

ROGER.
I SPEND MY DAYS JUST MOONING
SO SAD AND BLUE
I SPEND MY NIGHTS JUST MOONING
ALL OVER YOU.
JAN.
ALL OVER WHO?
ROGER.
OH, I'M SO FULL OF LOVE

AS ANY FOOL CAN SEE
'CAUSE ANGELS UP ABOVE HAVE HUNG A MOON ON ME.
I'LL STAND BEHIND YOU MOONING
FOR EVERMORE
    JAN.
FOR EVERMORE
    ROGER.
SOMEDAY YOU'LL FIND ME MOONING
AT YOUR FRONT DOOR
    JAN.
AT MY FRONT DOOR
    ROGER.
OH, EVERY DAY AT SCHOOL I WATCH YA
ALWAYS WILL UNTIL I GOTCHA
MOONING, TOO
THERE'S A MOON OUT TONIGHT

DOODY. Hey, Danny, there's that chick you know.

(SANDY and EUGENE enter. EUGENE wearing Bermuda shorts and argyle socks. They both have fishnet bags with leaves. RIZZO and KENICKIE sit up to look. DANNY moves to EUGENE and stares him down.)

EUGENE. Well, Sandy, I think I have all the leaves I want. Uh ... why don't I wait for you with dad in the station wagon.

(DANNY looking at EUGENE outlines a square with jerking head movement. EUGENE exits. As DANNY walks away, SONNY crosses to SANDY.)

SONNY. Hi ya, Sandy. What's shakin? How 'bout a Coke?
SANDY. No, thanks, I can't stay.
DANNY. Oh yeah? Then whattaya doin' hangin' around?
SANDY. I just came out to collect some leaves for biology.
SONNY. There's some really neat yellow ones over by the drainage canal. Come on, I'll show you.

(SONNY grabs SANDY and goes offstage.)

DOODY. Hey, Danny ... ain't you gonna follow 'em?

DANNY. Why should I? She don't mean nothin' to me.

RIZZO. Sure, Zuko, every day now! Ya mean you ain't told 'em?

KENICKIE. Come off it Rizzo. Whattaya' tryin' to do, make us think she's like you?

RIZZO. What's that crack supposed to mean? I ain't heard you complainin'.

KENICKIE. That's 'cause you never stop flappin' your gums!

DANNY. Hey, cool it, huh?

RIZZO. Shut up Kenickie or you're gonna get a knuckle sandwich.

KENICKIE. Oh, I'm really worried, scab!

RIZZO. Okay, you creep!

(She pushes him off bench and they fight on ground.)

ROGER and DOODY. Fight! Fight! Yaaayy! *(Etc.)*

(Various adlibs from GUYS and GIRLS: "Fight!" "What's happening?" "Crazy!" "Jeez" ... etc.)

DANNY. *(Separating them.)* Come on, cut it out! What a couple of fruitcakes!

RIZZO. Well, he started it!

KENICKIE. Man, what a yo-yo! Make one little joke, the chick goes tutti-fruitti!

DANNY. *(Glaring at RIZZO and KENICKIE.)* Cool it!

DOODY. Jeez, nice couple.

(There is an uncomfortable pause onstage as the kids hear VINCE FONTAINE on radio.)

VINCE'S VOICE. ... 'cause tomorrow night yours truly, the main-brain, Vince Fontaine, will be M.C.ing the big dance bash out at Rydell High School—in the boys' gym. And along with me will be Mr. T.N.T. himself, Johnny Casino and the Gamblers. So, make it a point to stop by the joint, Rydell High, 7:30 tomorrow night.

RIZZO. Hey, Danny, you going to the dance tomorrow night?

DANNY. I don't think so.

RIZZO. No? Aww, you're all broke up over little Gidget!

DANNY. Who?

RIZZO. Ahh, c'mon, Zuko, why don'tcha take me to the

dance—I can pull that Sandra Dee routine too. Right, you guys?

Song: "LOOK AT ME, I'M SANDRA DEE"

RIZZO.
LOOK AT ME, I'M SANDRA DEE
GODDESS OF ALL PURITY
WON'T BE MISLED
TRUST MY HEART, USE MY HEAD
I MUST, I'M SANDRA DEE
I DON'T LIE OR SWEAR
I DON'T RAT MY HAIR
I GET ILL AT THE SIGHT OF BLOOD
WELL, I DON'T CARE . . .
IF YOU THINK I'M SQUARE
FAIL IN SCHOOL
MY NAME WOULD BE MUD

(SANDY and SONNY enter, hearing the last part of the song. SONNY is behind her.)

OH, NO, NO SAL MINEO
I WOULD NEVER STOOP SO LOW
PLEASE KEEP YOUR COOL, NOW YOU'RE STARTING TO
     DROOL ... YOU FOOL!
I'M SANDRA DEE

(SANDY crosses to RIZZO.)

SONNY. Hey, Sandy, wait a minute. Hey ....
SANDY. *(To RIZZO.)* Listen, just who do you think you are? I saw you making fun of me. *(SANDY leaps on RIZZO and the two girls start fighting. DANNY pulls SANDY off.)* LET GO OF ME! YOU DIRTY LIAR! DON'T TOUCH ME!
RIZZO. Aaahh, let me go. I ain't gonna do nothin' to her. That chick's flipped her lid!

(SONNY and ROGER hold RIZZO.)

SANDY. You tell them right now that all those things you've been saying about me were lies. Go on, tell 'em.

DANNY. Whattaya talkin' about? I never said anything about you.

SANDY. You creep! You think you're such a big man don't ya? Trying to make me look cheap in front of your friends. I don't know why I ever liked you, Danny Zuko!

(SANDY runs off in tears. DANNY starts after her ... gives up.)

DANNY. Sandy!!!!!!!!!!!! *(Slowly turning to the others— Pause.)* Weird chick! *(Pause.)* Hey, Rizzo. You wanna go to the dance with me?

RIZZO. Huh? Yeah, sure. Why not? (move off)

ROGER. Hey, Jan. You got a date for the dance tomorrow night?

JAN. Tomorrow? Let me see— *(She takes out a little notebook and thumbs through it.)* No, I don't. Why?

ROGER. You wanna go with me?

JAN. You kiddin' me? Yeah, sure, Roge!

DOODY. Hey, French?

FRENCHY. Yeah?

DOODY. *(Very shy, moving to FRENCHY.)* Hey, Frenchy, can you still go to the dance, now that you quit school?

FRENCHY. Yeah, I guess so. Why?

DOODY. Oh.... Ahh, nothin' ...... I'll see ya there.

SONNY. Hey, Kenickie, how 'bout givin' me a ride tomorrow, and I'll pick us up a couple of dames at the dance.

DANNY. With what? A meat hook?

KENICKIE. Nah, I got a blind date from cross town. I hear she's a real bombshell.

MARTY. Gee, I don't even know if I'll go.

DANNY. Why not, Marty?

MARTY. I ain't got a date.

DANNY. Hey, I know just the guy. Right you guys!

(They yell offstage.)

ALL GUYS. Hey, Eugene!

(MARTY starts to chase DANNY, hitting him with magazine.)

Song: "WE GO TOGETHER"

ALL.
WE GO TOGETHER, LIKE
RAMA-LAMA-LAMA, KA-KINGA DA DING-DONG
REMEMBERED FOREVER, AS
SHOO-BOP SHA WADDA WADDA
YIPPITY BOOM-DE-BOOM
CHANG CHANG CHANGITTY-CHANG SHOO BOP
THAT'S THE WAY IT SHOULD BE (WHAA-OOHH! YEAH!)

WE'RE ONE OF A KIND, LIKE DIP-DA-DIP-DA-DIP
DOO WOP DA DOOBY DOO
OUR NAMES ARE SIGNED
BOOGEDY, BOOGEDY, BOOGEDY, BOOGEDY, SHOOBY-DO
    WOP-SHE-BOP
CHANG CHANG-A CHANGITTY CHANG SHOO BOP
WE'LL ALWAYS BE LIKE ONE (WHAA-WHA-WHA-
    WHAAAAAH)

WHEN WE GO OUT AT NIGHT
AND STARS ARE SHINING BRIGHT
UP IN THE SKIES ABOVE
OR AT THE HIGH SCHOOL DANCE
WHERE YOU CAN FIND ROMANCE
MAYBE IT MIGHT BE LA-A-A-AH-OVE!

(Riff chorus.)

WE'RE FOR EACH OTHER, LIKE
A WOP BABA LU MOP AHH WOP BAM BOOM!
JUST LIKE MY BROTHER, IS
SHA NA NA NA NA NA YIPPITY DIP DE DOOM
CHANG CHANG-A CHANGITTY CHANG SHOO BOP
WE'LL ALWAYS BE TOGETHER!

*(At the end of the song, the lights fade on the KIDS as they go off
    laughing and horsing around.)*

END OF ACT ONE

ACT II

Scene 1

VINCE FONTAINE'S RADIO VOICE. Hey, it's the Main Brain Vince Fontaine. Got my umbrella 'cause it's starting to rain. If it's cloudy and blue where you are too, 'cause the boy you love doesn't love you. Here's one for the lonely from your one and only. Yep. It's Raining on Prom Night.

(Lights come up and SANDY, in her bathrobe, is revealed in her bedroom. She turns up the volume on radio.)

Song: "IT'S RAINING ON PROM NIGHT"

(Song comes on radio. SANDY sings lead vocal with the FEMALE RADIO VOICE in harmony.)

RADIO VOICE.
I WAS DEPRIVED OF A YOUNG GIRLS DREAM
BY THE CRUEL FORCE OF NATURE FROM THE BLUE ...
    SANDY.
INSTEAD OF A NIGHT FULL OF ROMANCE SUPREME
ALL I GOT WAS A RUNNY NOSE AND ASIATIC FLU
IT'S RAINING ON PROM NIGHT
MY HAIR IS A MESS
IT'S RUNNING ALL OVER MY TAFFETA DRESS
IT'S RAINING, AND STAINING
MY WHITE SATIN PUMPS
AND MASCARA FLOWS, RIGHT DOWN MY NOSE
I'M DOWN IN THE DUMPS
I DON'T EVEN HAVE MY CORSAGE, OH GEE
IT FELL DOWN THE SEWER WITH MY SISTER'S ID

(SANDY talks verse while RADIO VOICE continues to sing.)

YES, IT'S RAINING ON PROM NIGHT
OH, WHAT CAN I DO? I MISS YOU
IT'S RAINING RAIN FROM THE SKIES
IT'S RAINING TEARS FROM MY EYES OVER YOU.

Dear God, let him feel the same way I do right now. Make him want
to see me again! *(SANDY resumes singing the lead.)*

IT'S RAINING ON PROM NIGHT
OH, WHAT CAN I DO?
IT'S RAINING RAIN FROM THE SKIES
IT'S RAINING TEARS FROM MY EYES
OVER YOU—OOO-OOO-OOO—RAIN-ING.

*(After the song ends "Shakin' at the High School Hop" begins. Lights
fade out on SANDY and come up on the high school dance. The
couples are: DANNY and RIZZO, JAN and ROGER, FRENCHY
and DOODY. MISS LYNCH is overseeing the punchbowl.
MARTY is alone and SONNY is in the corner. JOHNNY CASINO,
with guitar, on bandstand.)*

Song: "SHAKIN' AT THE HIGH SCHOOL HOP"

JOHNNY CASINO and ENSEMBLE.
WELL, HONKY-TONK BABY, GET ON THE FLOOR
ALL THE CATS ARE SHOUTIN', THEY'RE YELLIN' FOR MORE
MY BABY LIKES TO ROCK, MY BABY LIKES TO ROLL
MY BABY DOES THE CHICKEN AND SHE DOES THE STROLL
WELL THEY SHAKE IT
OH, SHAKE IT
YEAH, SHAKE IT
EVERYBODY SHAKIN'
SHAKIN' AT THE HIGH SCHOOL HOP

GIRLS.
WELL, WE'RE GONNA ALLEY-OOOP ON BLUEBERRY HILL
GUYS.
HULLY-GULLY WITH LUCILLE, WON'T BE STANDING STILL

GIRLS.
HAND-JIVE BABY
   ALL.
DO THE STOMP WITH ME
I CHA-LYPSO, DO THE SLOP, GONNA BOP WITH MR. LEE
WELL, THEY SHAKE IT
OH, SHAKE IT
YEAH, SHAKE IT,
EVERYBODY'S SHAKIN'
SHAKIN' AT THE HIGH SCHOOL HOP

SHAKE, ROCK AND ROLL
ROCK, ROLL AND SHAKE
SHAKE, ROCK AND ROLL
ROCK, ROLL AND SHAKE
SHAKE, ROCK AND ROLL
SHAKIN' AT THE HIGH SCHOOL HOP

(DANCE BREAK.)

SHAKE, ROCK AND ROLL
ROCK, ROLL AND SHAKE
SHAKE, ROCK AND ROLL
ROCK, ROLL AND SHAKE
SHAKE, ROCK AND ROLL
SHAKIN' AT THE HIGH SCHOOL HOP

(At the end of "Shakin'" the KIDS cheer and yell.) (Front & center)

VINCE. *(Enters and grabs microphone.)* Alright, Johnny Casino and the Gamblers! I've had a request for a slow one. How about it, Johnny Casino?

JOHNNY CASINO. Okay, Vince, here's a little number I wrote called "Enchanted Guitar."

VINCE. And don't forget, only ten more minutes 'til the big Hand-Jive dance contest. So, if you've got a steady, get her ready.

RIZZO. Hey, Danny, you gonna be my partner for the dance contest?

DANNY. Maybe, if nothing better comes along.

RIZZO. Drop dead!   move to the back
ROGER. OW!

JAN. Sorry.

ROGER. Why don'tcha let me lead for a change?

JAN. I can't help it, I'm used to leading

FRENCHY. Hey, Doody, can't you at least turn me around or somethin'?

DOODY. Don't talk, I'm tryin' to count.

(PATTY dances near DANNY with EUGENE.) ⭐

PATTY. Danny! Danny!

DANNY. Yeah, that's my name, don't wear it out.

PATTY. How did the track tryouts go?

DANNY. I made the team.

PATTY. Oh, wonderful!

RIZZO. Hey, Zuko, I think she's tryin' to tell ya somethin'! Go on, dance with her. You ain't doin' me no good.

DANNY. Hey, Eugene, Betty Rizzo thinks you look like Pat Boone.

EUGENE. Oh?

(EUGENE walks over and stands near RIZZO, staring. He polishes his white bucks on the backs of his pants legs. DANNY dances with PATTY.)

RIZZO. Whattaya say, Fruit Boots?

(Music tempo changes to cha-cha. KENICKIE and CHA-CHA DeGREGORIO enter.)

CHA-CHA. Jeez, nice time to get here. Look, the joint's half empty already

KENICKIE. Ahh, knock it off! Can I help it if my car wouldn't start?

CHA-CHA. Jeez, what crummy decorations!

KENICKIE. Where'd ya think you were goin', American Bandstand?

CHA-CHA. We had a sock-hop at St. Bernadette's once. The sisters got real pumpkins and everything.

KENICKIE. Neat. They probably didn't have a Bingo game that night.

(The song ends and KIDS cheer. JOHNNY CASINO looks for VINCE

FONTAINE on the dance floor.)

JOHNNY CASINO. Hey, Vince .... any more requests?

VINCE. Yeah, play anything!

JOHNNY CASINO. Okay, here's a little tune called "Anything!"

PATTY. *(Still dancing with DANNY.)* I can't imagine you ever having danced with Sandy like this.

DANNY. Whattaya mean?

PATTY. I mean her being so clumsy and all. She can't even twirl a baton right. In fact, I've been thinking of having a little talk with the coach about her.

DANNY. Why? Whatta you care?

PATTY. Well, I mean ... even you have to admit she's a bit of a drip. I mean ... isn't that why you broke up with her?

DANNY. Hey, listen ...... y'know she used to be a half-way decent chick before she got mixed up with you and your brown-nose friends.

(DANNY walks away from her. PATTY, stunned, runs to the punch table. KENICKIE walks up to RIZZO.)

RIZZO. Hey, Kenickie, where ya been, the submarine races?

KENICKIE. Nah. I had to go to Egypt to pick up a date.

RIZZO. You feel like dancin'?

KENICKIE. Crazy.

EUGENE. It's been very nice talking to you, Betty.

RIZZO. Yeah, see ya around the Bookmobile.

(KENICKIE and RIZZO dance off.)

VINCE. *(Doing the cha-cha with MARTY.)* I'm Vince Fontaine. Do your folks know that I come into your room every night??? Over WAXX, that is! *(VINCE laughs.)* I'm gonna judge the dance contest. Are you gonna be in it?

MARTY. I guess not. I ain't got a date.

VINCE. What? A knockout like you? Things sure have changed since I went to school .... last year.

DOODY. *(Pointing at CHA-CHA.)* Hey, ain't that the chick Kenickie walked in with?

SONNY. Where?

DOODY. The one pickin' her nose over there.

SONNY. That's the baby. I thought she was one of the cafeteria ladies.

CHA-CHA. *(Standing near EUGENE.)* Hey, did you come here to dance or didn't ya?

EUGENE. Of course, but I never learned how to do this dance.

CHA-CHA. Ahh, there's nothing to it. I'm gonna teach "ballroom" at the CYO. *(She grabs EUGENE in dance position.)* Now, one-two-cha-cha-cha, three-four-cha-cha-cha-very good-cha-cha-cha-keep-it-up-cha-cha-cha.......

EUGENE. You certainly dance well.

CHA-CHA. Thanks, you can hold me a little tighter. I won't bite cha.

(CHA-CHA grabs EUGENE in a bear hug. Music ends and KIDS applaud.)

JOHNNY CASINO. Thank you. This is Johnny Casino telling you when you hear the tone it will be exactly one minute to HAND-JIVE TIME!

(Excited murmurs and scrambling for partners takes place on the dance floor as the band's guitarist makes a "twang" sound on his "E" string.)

EUGENE. Excuse me, it was very nice meeting you.

CHA-CHA. Hey, wait a minute .... don'tcha want my phone number or somethin'?

EUGENE. *(Crosses to PATTY.)* Patty, you promised to be my partner for the dance contest, remember?

PATTY. That's right. I almost forgot.

(EUGENE pulls her away.)

DANNY. Hey, Rizzo. I'm ready to dance with you now.

RIZZO. Don't strain yourself ..... I'm dancin' with Kenickie.

KENICKIE. That's all right, Zuko, you can have my date. *(He yells.)* Hey, Charlene! Come 'ere!

CHA-CHA. *(She crosses over.)* Yeah? Whattaya want?

DANNY. Are you kiddin' me?

KENICKIE. How'dja like to dance this next one with Danny Zuko?

T-Birds

CHA-CHA. The big wheel of the ~~Burger Palace Boys~~. I didn't even know he saw me here.

DANNY. I didn't!

(Other GUYS laugh.)

JOHNNY CASINO. Okay, alligators, here it is. The big one ..... the Hand Jive Dance Contest. *(KIDS cheer.)* Let's get things under way by bringing up our very own Miss Lynch.

(KIDS react.)

MISS LYNCH. Thank you, Clarence. *(CROWD starts laughing and yelling.)* Whenever you're finished. Before we begin, I'd like to welcome you all to "Moonlight in the Tropics." And I think we all owe a big round of applause to Patty Simcox and her committee for the wonderful decorations.

(Mixed reaction from CROWD.)

EUGENE. Yay, Patty!

MISS LYNCH. Now, I'm sure, you'll be glad to know that I'm not judging this dance contest. *(Few KIDS cheer.)* All right. I'd like to present Mr. Vince Fontaine. Mr. Fontaine? .... Mr. Fontaine?

VINCE. Comin' right up!

MISS LYNCH. As most of you know, Mr. Fontaine is an announcer for radio station WAXX. *(VINCE, on the bandstand, whispers in her ear.)* ... uh ... *(Uncomfortably.)* "Dig the scene on big fifteen." *(Cheer goes up.)* Now for the rules! One: All couples must be boy-girl.

ROGER. Too bad, Eugene!

MISS LYNCH. Two: If Mr. Fontaine taps you on the shoulder, you must clear the dance floor immediately....

VINCE. *(Grabbing the mike from MISS LYNCH.)* I just wanna say, truly in all sincerity, Miss Lynch, that you're doing a really, really terrific job here, terrific. And I'll sure bet these kids are lucky to have you for a teacher, 'cause I'll bet in all sincerity that you're really terrific. IS SHE TERRIFIC KIDS? *(The KIDS cheer.)* And some lucky guy and gal is gonna go boppin' home with a stack of terrific prizes. But don't feel bad if I bump yuzz out, 'cause it don't matter if you win or lose, it's what ya do with those dancing shoes.

So, okay, cats, throw your mittens around your kittens ... and AWAY WE GO!

(VINCE does Jackie Gleason pose. JOHNNY CASINO sings "Born to Hand-Jive." During the dance, couples are eliminated one by one as VINCE FONTAINE mills through the crowd, tapping each couple.)

Song: "BORN TO HAND-JIVE"

JOHNNY CASINO.
BEFORE I WAS BORN, LATE ONE NIGHT
MY PAPA SAID, EVERYTHING'S ALL RIGHT
THE DOCTOR LAUGHED WHEN MA LAID DOWN
WITH HER STOMACH BOUNCIN' ALL AROUND
'CAUSE A BE-BOP STORK WAS 'BOUT TO ARRIVE
AND MAMA GAVE BIRTH TO THE HAND-JIVE

I COULD BARELY WALK WHEN I MILKED A COW
WHEN I WAS THREE I PUSHED A PLOW
WHILE CHOPPIN' WOOD I'D MOVE MY LEGS
AND STARTED DANCIN' WHILE I GATHERED EGGS
TOWN FOLK CLAPPED, I WAS ONLY FIVE
HE'LL OUT DANCE 'EM ALL, HE'S A BORN "HAND-JIVE"

(DANCE BREAK.)

BORN TO HAND-JIVE, BABEEEEEEEEEE!!!!!!!!!
BORN TO HAND-JIVE, BABY!!!!!!!!

(DANCE BREAK.)

NOW, CAN YOU HAND-JIVE, BABEEEEEEEEEEEE??!!
OH, CAN YOU HAND-JIVE, BABY?
OH YEAH, OH YEAH, OH YEAH.

JOHNNY CASINO and COMPANY.
BORN TO HAND-JIVE, OH YEAH!!!!!!!!!!!

MISS LYNCH. *(Out of breath on bandstand.)* My Goodness!

Well, we have our winners. Will you step up here for your prizes. Daniel Zuko and ....

CHA-CHA. Cha-Cha DiGregorio

MISS LYNCH. Uh ..… Cha-Cha DiGregorio.

CHA-CHA. They call me Cha-Cha 'cause I'm the best dancer at St. Bernadettes.

RYDELL KIDS. Boooooooooooooo!

MISS LYNCH. Oh .... that's very nice. Congratulations to the both of you, and here are your prizes: Two free passes to the Twi-Light Drive-In Theatre ... good on any week night. *(KIDS cheer.)* A coupon worth ten dollars off at Robert Hall. *(KIDS boo.)* And last but not least, your trophies, prepared by Mrs. Schneider's art class.

(Cheers and applause. MISS LYNCH presents DANNY and CHA-CHA with two hideous ceramic nebbishes in dance positions, mounted on blocks of wood.)

VINCE. *(Grabbing the mike from MISS LYNCH.)* Weren't they terrific? C'mon, let's hear it for these kids! *(KIDS cheer.)* Only thing I wanna say before we wrap things up is that you kids at Rydell are the greatest!

RYDELL KIDS. YEAH! YAY! etc.

VINCE. Last dance, ladies choice.

(Band plays slow instrumental. Couples leave dance, one by one until CHA-CHA is left alone as PATTY, EUGENE and MISS LYNCH clean after dance. Each exits as the lights change to new scene.)

(hopelessly devoted)

Scene 2

SCENE: It is evening a few days later in front of the Burger Palace. FRENCHY is pacing around, magazine in hand, looking at sign on Burger Palace window: "Counter Girl Wanted." After a few moments SONNY, KENICKIE and DOODY enter with weapons: DOODY with a baseball bat, SONNY with a zip-gun, KENICKIE with a lead pipe and chain. They wear leather jackets and engineer boots.

KENICKIE. Hey, Sonny, what Cracker-Jack box ja' get that zip gun out of, anyway?

SONNY. What do you mean, I made it in shop. Hey, what's shakin', French? You get out of beauty school already?

FRENCHY. Oh ..... I cut tonight. Those beauty teachers they got workin' there don't know nothin'. Hey, what's with the arsenal?

DOODY. We gotta rumble with the Flaming Dukes.

FRENCHY. No lie! How come?

KENICKIE. Remember that scuzzy chick I took to the dance?

DOODY. Godzilla!

DOODY and KENICKIE. *(Imitating EUGENE and CHA-CHA dancing.)* "One-two-Cha-Cha-Cha!"

SONNY. Well, it turns out she goes steady with the leader of the Flaming Dukes. And, she told this guy that Danny tried to put his hands all over her.

KENICKIE. If he did, he musta been makin' a bug collection for Biology.

FRENCHY. *(Seeing DANNY.)* Hey, look .... ain't that Danny?

DOODY. Hey, Danny!

FRENCHY. What's he doing in his underwear?

(DANNY enters in a white track suit carrying a relay race baton.)

DOODY. That's a track suit! Hi ya, Danny.

KENICKIE. Whoa, Zuko! Where do you keep your "Wheaties?"

DANNY. Ha, ha! Big joke!

SONNY. Hey, it's a good thing you're here. We're supposed to rumble the Dukes tonight!

DANNY. What time?

KENICKIE. 9:00.

DANNY. Nice play! I got field training 'til 9:30.

KENICKIE. Can't you sneak away, man?

DANNY. Not a chance! The coach'd give me a boot in the keyster.

SONNY and KENICKIE. The coach!

DANNY. Besides, what am I supposed to do, stomp on somebody's face with my *gym* shoes.

KENICKIE. Ahh, c'mon Zuko, whattaya tryin' to prove with this track team garbage.

DANNY. Why? Whattaya care? Look, I gotta cut. I'm in the middle of a race right now. See ya later.

(DANNY starts off.)

SONNY. You got "the hots" for that cheerleader or somethin'? *(DANNY stops, turns head and stares SONNY down. DANNY exits.)* Neat guy, causes a ruckus and then he cuts out on us!

KENICKIE. Jeez, next thing ya' know he'll be gettin' a crew cut!

DOODY. Nah. He'd look neater with a flat top!

FRENCHY. Yeah, with a D.A. in the back and some Brillcreme going through it. "A little dab'll do ya!"

KENICKIE. Hey Frenchy, you better scram. Before you get hurt.

FRENCHY. *(Looking at DOODY.)* I am getting kinda hungry.

(DOODY nods and motions for her to go inside the Burger Palace. She exits.)

SONNY. Looks like they ain't gonna show. They said they'd be here at nine.

DOODY. What time is it?

SONNY. *(Looking at his watch.)* It's almost five after ...... c'mon let's split.

KENICKIE. Give 'em time, they'll be here. Hey, whatever happened to Rump?

SONNY. Who cares about Tubby? Who'da ever thought Zuko'd punk out on us.

KENICKIE. Nice rumble! A herd of Flaming Dukes against you, me and Howdy Doody.

ROGER. *(Charging on with car antenna in hand.)* OHHHHHHH, KAY! Where the heck are they? Hey, where's Zuko?

SONNY. Well, look who's here. Where you been, Pizza Face?

ROGER. Hey, right here, Rum-Dum! My old man made me help him paint the stupid basement. I couldn't even find my bullwhip. I had to bust off an aerial.

KENICKIE. Ha, whattaya expect to do with that thing?

ROGER. Oh yeah, Kenickie. I'll take this over any of *those* Tinker Toys!

(He lashes the air above KENICKIE's head, almost hitting SONNY behind him.)

SONNY. Hey, watch it with that thing, Pimple Puss!

ROGER. Hey, whatsa matter, LaTierri, afraid you might get hurt a little?

SONNY. Listen, Blubber Boy, you're gonna look real funny cruisin' around the neighborhood in an iron lung.

ROGER. Well, why don'tcha use that thing, then? You got enough rubber bands there to start three paper routes.

KENICKIE. *(Grabbing DOODY's baseball bat.)* Hey, Rump! C'mon let's see ya try that again.

ROGER. What'sa matter, Kenicks? What happened to your big bad pipe? Huh!? Huh!?

KENICKIE. No Sonny, don't shoot! *(ROGER turns and KENICKIE knocks the antenna from his hand.)* Okay, Rump, how's about mooning the Flaming Dukes? Pants 'em!

(Miscellaneous adlibs! Hoots and hollers! "Get 'em!" etc. SONNY and KENICKIE leap on ROGER and get his pants off. DOODY helps with the shoes. SONNY and KENICKIE run off with ROGER'S pants as DOODY gathers up weapons.)

DOODY. Hey, you guys, wait up!

(DOODY starts to run off, then goes back to hand ROGER his antenna. DOODY exits.)

FRENCHY. *(Walks out of Burger Palace and sees ROGER in loud silly boxer shorts. She screams.)* AHHHHHHHHHHHHH!

ROGER. *(Turns and in embarrassment runs off after GUYS.)* AHHHHHHHHHHH!

FRENCHY. Jeez! What am I gonna do? I mean, I can't just tell everybody I dropped out of beauty school. I can't get a job in the Burger Palace. Not with those guys always hangin' around. Boy, I wish I had one of those Guardian Angel things like in that Debbie Reynolds movie. Would that be neat. Somebody always there to tell you what's the best thing to do.

(Spooky angelic guitar chords. FRENCHY's GUARDIAN TEEN ANGEL appears swinging in quietly on a rope. He is a Fabian-like rock singer. White Fabian sweater with the collar turned up, white chinos, white boots, a large white comb sticking out of his pocket. He sings "Beauty School Dropout." After the first verse, a chorus of ANGELS appears: a group of girls in white plastic sheets and their hair in white plastic rollers in a halo effect. They

provide background doo-wahs. The TEEN ANGEL sings.)

Song: "BEAUTY SCHOOL DROPOUT"

TEEN ANGEL.
YOUR STORY'S SAD TO TELL
A TEENAGE NE'ER-DO-WELL
MOST MIXED-UP NON-DELINQUENT ON THE BLOCK
YOUR FUTURE'S SO UNCLEAR NOW
WHAT'S LEFT OF YOUR CAREER NOW
CAN'T EVEN GET A TRADE-IN ON YOUR SMOCK

(Scrim rises slowly with music as a spotlight bumps on TEEN ANGEL and the heavenly CHORUS.)

BEAUTY SCHOOL DROPOUT
NO GRADUATION DAY FOR YOU
BEAUTY SCHOOL DROPOUT
MISSED YOUR MID-TERMS AND FLUNKED SHAMPOO
WELL, AT LEAST YOU COULD HAVE TAKEN TIME
TO WASH AND CLEAN YOUR CLOTHES UP
AFTER SPENDING ALL THAT DOUGH TO HAVE
THE DOCTOR FIX YOUR NOSE UP

BABY, GET MOVIN'
WHY KEEP YOUR FEEBLE HOPES ALIVE?
WHAT ARE YOU PROVIN'?
YOU GOT THE DREAM BUT NOT THE DRIVE
IF YOU GO FOR YOUR DIPLOMA YOU COULD JOIN A STENO
POOL
TURN IN YOUR TEASING COMB AND GO BACK TO HIGH
SCHOOL

BEAUTY SCHOOL DROPOUT
HANGIN' AROUND THE CORNER STORE
BEAUTY SCHOOL DROPOUT
IT'S ABOUT TIME YOU KNEW THE SCORE
WELL, THEY COULDN'T TEACH YOU ANYTHING
YOU THINK IT'S SUCH A BOTHER
BUT NO CUSTOMER WOULD GO TO YOU

UNLESS IT WAS YOUR FATHER
BABY, DON'T SWEAT IT
YOU'RE NOT CUT OUT TO HOLD A JOB
BETTER FORGET IT
WHO WANTS THEIR HAIR DONE BY A SLOB?
NOW YOUR BANGS ARE CURLED, YOUR LASHES TWIRLED,
BUT STILL THE WORLD IS CRUEL
WIPE OFF THAT ANGEL FACE AND GO BACK TO HIGH
     SCHOOL.

*(At the end of the verse the TEEN ANGEL hands FRENCHY a high
school diploma, which she uncurls, looks at, crumples up and
throws away. The TEEN ANGEL and CHOIR look on. FRENCHY
walks away.)*

BABY, YA BLEW IT
YOU PUT OUR GOOD ADVICE TO SHAME
HOW COULD YOU DO IT?
BETCHA DEAR ABBY'D SAY THE SAME.
GUESS THERE'S NO WAY TO GET THROUGH TO YOU
NO MATTER WHO MAY TRY
MIGHT AS WELL GO BACK TO THAT MALT SHOP IN THE SKY.

(CHOIR exits and TEEN ANGEL swings off on rope.)

Scene 3

*SCENE: Scene comes up on Greased Lightning at the Twi-Light
Drive-In Theatre. SANDY and DANNY are sitting alone wearing
3-D glasses at opposite ends of the front seat staring straight
ahead in awkward silence. Movie music is coming out of a
portable speaker. Dialogue from the movie begins to come out of
the speaker over eerie background music.*

GIRL'S VOICE. It was ….. like an animal ….. with awful
clawing hands and ….. and ….. hideous fangs ….. oh, it was like a
nightmare!
    HERO'S VOICE. There, there, you're safe now, Sheila.
    SCIENTIST'S VOICE. Poor Todd. The radiation has caused

him to mutate. He's become half man, half monster ... like a werewolf.

SHEILA'S VOICE. But, doctor, he ... he's my brother. And his big stock car race is tomorrow!

(Werewolf howl.)

HERO'S VOICE. Great Scott! It's a full moon!

DANNY. *(Removing his glasses.)* Why don'tcha move over a little closer?

SANDY. This is all right.

DANNY. Well, can't ya at least smile or somethin'? Look, Sandy, I practically had to bust Kenickie's arm to get his car for tonight. The guys are really P.O.'ed at me. I mean, I thought we were gonna forget about that scene in the park with Sonny and Rizzo and everything. I told ya on the phone I was sorry.

SANDY. I know you did.

DANNY. Well? *(Pause.)* Hey, you ain't goin' with another guy, are ya?

SANDY. No. Why?

DANNY. Err ... oh, ah ... nothin' .... well, yeah.... *(DANNY tries to take off his ring.)* I was gonna ask ya to take my ring.

SANDY. Oh, Danny ... I don't know what to say.

DANNY. Well, don'tcha want it?

SANDY. Uh-huh.

(He puts it on her finger. She kisses him on the cheek.)

DANNY. All right! *(Beeps car horn.)* I shoulda gave it to ya' a long time ago. I really like you, Sandy.

(He attempts to kiss her on the lips.)

SANDY. Danny, take it easy! What are you trying to do?

DANNY. Whattsa' matter?

SANDY. Well, I mean ..... I thought we were just gonna—you know—be steadies.

DANNY. Well, whattaya' think going steady is, anyway? C'mon Sandy!

SANDY. Stop it! I've never seen you like this.

DANNY. Whattaya gettin' so shook up about? I thought I meant somethin' to ya.

    SANDY. You do. But I'm still the same girl I was last summer. Just because you give me your ring doesn't mean you can do whatever you want.

(SANDY opens the car door, gets out.)

    DANNY. Hey, Sandy, wait a minute.

(SANDY slams car door on DANNY's hand.)

    SANDY. I'm sorry, Danny ....
    DANNY. *(In pain, falsetto voice.)* It's nothing!
    SANDY. Maybe we better just forget about it.

(SANDY tries to give DANNY his ring back. When he refuses, she leaves it on car's hood. She exits.)

    DANNY. Hey, Sandy, where you goin'? You can't just walk out of a drive-in!
    HERO'S VOICE. Look Sheila! The full moon is sinking behind "Dead Man's Curve."

(DANNY gets out of car to get ring.)

    SHEILA'S VOICE. Yes, Lance ... and with it ... all our dreams.

(Werewolf howl.
DANNY sings "Alone at a Drive-In Movie" with werewolf howls coming from movie and the BURGER PALACE BOYS offstage singing background doo-wops in DANNY's mind.)

        Song: "ALONE AT A DRIVE-IN MOVIE"

    Sandy

    DANNY.
I'M ... ALL ... ALONE
AT THE DRIVE-IN MOVIE
IT'S A FEELIN' THAT AIN'T TOO GROOVY.
WATCHIN' WEREWOLVES WITHOUT YOU.

(Offstage howls.)

AND WHEN THE INTERMISSION ELF
MOVES THE CLOCK'S HANDS
WHILE HE'S EATING EVERYTHING
SOLD AT THE STAND

WHEN THERE'S ONE MINUTE TO GO
TILL THE LIGHTS GO DOWN LOW
I'LL BE HOLDING THE SPEAKER KNOBS
MISSING YOU SOOOOOOOOOOOO!!!!!

I CAN'T BELIEVE IT
UNSTEAMED WINDOWS I CAN SEE THROUGH
MIGHT AS WELL BE IN AN IGLOO
'CAUSE THE HEATER DOESN'T WORK
AS ... GOOD ... AS ... YOU!!!!!!!!!!!!

OFFSTAGE GUYS.
BABY, COME BACK !!!!!!!!!!!!!!

(Lights fade on DANNY as he drives off in car.)

Scene 4

SCENE: A party in JAN's basement. ROGER and DOODY sitting on barstools singing "Rock 'n Roll Party Queen" accompanied by DOODY's guitar. KENICKIE and RIZZO are dancing. SONNY and MARTY are on the couch tapping feet and drinking Cokes. FRENCHY is sitting on floor next to record player keeping time to the music. JAN is swaying to the music. SANDY sits alone on stairs trying to fit in and enjoy herself. DANNY is not present.

(stage right)

Song: "ROCK 'N ROLL PARTY QUEEN"

DOODY and ROGER.
LITTLE GIRL— Y'KNOW WHO I MEAN
PRETTY SOON SHE'LL BE SEVENTEEN

THEY TELL ME HER NAME'S BETTY JEAN
THE HA-HA ROCK 'N ROLL PARTY QUEEN

FRIDAY NIGHT AND SHE'S GOT A DATE
GOIN' PLACES—JUSTA STAYIN' OUT LATE
DROPPIN' DIMES IN THE RECORD MACHINE
AH-HO-HO, ROCK 'N ROLL PARTY QUEEN.

PA-PA-PA-PA-PA, OH, NO
CAN I HAVE THE CAR TONIGHT?
BAY-BA BAY-BEE, CAN I BE THE ONE
TO LOVE YOU WITH ALL MY MIGHT (I-YI-YI-YI)

OH ROCKIN' AND AH ROLLIN' LITTLE PARTY QUEEN
WE GONNA DO THE STROLL, HEY PARTY QUEEN
KNOW I LOVE YOU SO, MY PARTY QUEEN
YOU'RE MY ROCKIN' AND MY ROLLIN' … PARTY QUEE-EEN!

SANDY. Don't put too many records on, Frenchy. I'm going to leave in a couple of minutes.

KENICKIE. Aah, come on! You ain't takin' your record player already! The party's just getting' started.

RIZZO. Yeah, she's cuttin out because Zuko ain't here.

SANDY. No, I'm not! I didn't come here to see him.

RIZZO. No? What'dja come for, then.

SANDY. Uh … because I was invited.

RIZZO. We only invited ya' because we needed a record player.

JAN. *(Trying to avoid trouble, motions to FRENCHY.)* Hey, French!

FRENCHY. Don't mind her, Sandy. C'mon. Let's go help Jan fix the food.

MARTY. Man, you're really a barrel of laughs tonight, Rizzo. What's buggin' you, anyway? *(grabs belly)*

RIZZO. Huh? Ah, never mind … it's a long story. *(Awkward pause.)* Hey, what happened to the music? Why don't you guys sing another song?

ROGER. O.K. Hey, hey, back by popular demand! Doody, let's do that new one by the Tinkletones.

DOODY and ROGER.
EACH NIGHT I CRY MYSELF TO SLEEP
THE GIRL I LOVE IS GONE FOR KEEPS …..

OOO-WA OOO-OOO-WA

(SANDY crosses with record player.)

RIZZO. Hey! Just a minute, Miss Goody-Two-Shoes! Where do you think you're going? *(SANDY looks around frightened then exits. RIZZO shouts after her.)* Hey, how come I didn't see Zuko here tonight?! You listening, Miss Sandra Dee......?!

(Lights fade out on party. Lights up on SANDY.)

[handwritten: There are worse things I could do (Spot down right)]

Song: "LOOK AT ME, I'M SANDRA DEE" (Reprise)

SANDY.
LOOK AT ME, THERE HAS TO BE
SOMETHING MORE THAN WHAT THEY SEE
WHOLESOME AND PURE, ALSO SCARED AND UNSURE
A POOR MAN'S SANDRA DEE

WHEN THEY CRITICIZE AND MAKE FUN OF ME
CAN'T THEY SEE THE TEARS IN MY SMILE?
DON'T THEY REALIZE THERE'S JUST ONE OF ME
AND IT HAS TO LAST ME A WHILE

(FRENCHY enters light.)

Hey, French? Can you come over to my house for awhile? And bring your makeup case, O.K.?

(Lights down on FRENCHY.)

SANDY, YOU MUST START ANEW
DON'T YOU KNOW WHAT YOU MUST DO?
HOLD YOUR HEAD HIGH
TAKE A DEEP BREATH AND CRY
GOODBYE
TO SANDRA DEE

(On last line of song she pulls the ribbon from her pony-tail and shakes her hair down.)

Scene 5

SCENE: Lights come up inside of the Burger Palace. ROGER,
DOODY, KENICKIE and SONNY are sitting at the counter.

ROGER. Hey, you guys wanna come over to my house and
watch the Mickey Mouse club?

(PATTY enters in cheerleader costume dragging pom poms
dispiritedly.)

KENICKIE. Hey, it's little Miss Pom-Poms! Why don't ya
make ME a big track star too?
SONNY. Nah, get me out on that field—by the cheerleaders—I
got WAY better moves than Zuko.
PATTY. You're disgusting, all of you!

(DANNY enters in letterman sweater, he wears horn-rimmed
glasses.)

DANNY. Hey, you guys!
SONNY. Whoa! Look at this!
DOODY. Hi ya, Danny!
KENICKIE. Zuko what happened to you?!!!!!!!!
DANNY. Wadda ya mean? I think I look cool! Right?
GUYS. *(Not convinced.)* Right.
ROGER. Hey, come on, we were just goin' over to my house to
watch the Mickey Mouse Club.
DANNY. Cool. Let's go.
PATTY. Danny, you look wonderful!!

(DANNY is momentarily distracted by PATTY.)

ROGER. Ahh, come on Zuko! Nobody's home.
DANNY. Solid! Later, Patty!

(GUYS start to leave. MARTY, FRENCHY, RIZZO and JAN in Pink
Ladies jackets enter silently, gesturing the guys to "be cool" as
they take up defiant positions. SANDY enters, now a Greaser's
"Dream Girl." A wild new hair style, black leather motorcycle

jacket with silver studs on the back that spell "BIG D," skin-tight slacks, gold hoop earrings. Yet, she actually looks prettier and more alive than she ever has.)

RIZZO. Remember, play it cool.

DANNY. Hey, Sandy! Wow, what a total! Wick-ed!

SANDY. What's it to ya, Zuko?

DANNY. Hey, we were just goin' to check out "The Mouseketeers." How would you like to come along?

PATTY. Danny, what's gotten into you? You couldn't possibly be interested in that ... that floozy.

(SANDY looks to RIZZO for her next move. Then she strolls over to PATTY, studies her calmly, and punches her in the eye. PATTY falls.)

PINK LADIES. YAA-AAY!

PATTY. Oh, my God, I'm going to have a black eye!

FRENCHY. *(Opening her purse.)* Don't sweat it, Patty. I'll fix it up. I just got a new job, demonstrating this miracle make-up at Woolworth's.

DANNY. Hey, Sandy, you're somethin' else!

SANDY. Oh, so ya' noticed, huh? Tell me about it ... Big Boy!

Song: ~~*"ALL CHOKED UP"*~~ You're the want

DANNY.
WELL, I FEEL SO STRANGE
WELL, UPON MY WORD
NOW MY BRAIN IS REELING
AND MY EYESIGHT'S BLURRED
I TREMBLE A LOT
I'M NERVOUS AND I'M HOT
UH-HUH! I'M ALL CHOKED UP

THERE'S A FIRE ALARM WAILIN' IN MY HEAD
AND MY CIRCULATION SAYS CONDITION RED
I'M IN A COLD SWEAT
MY T-SHIRTS ALL WET
UH-HUH! I'M ALL CHOKED UP

PINK LADIES.
NOW LISTEN HERE

SANDY.
SO YOU'RE SPINNIN' ROUND IN A DIZZY SPELL
IT'S A SITUATION I KNOW PRETTY WELL
YEAH, I'VE BEEN THERE TOO
SO I FEEL FOR YOU
UH-HUH! I'M ALL CHOKED UP!

OH, BABY, TAKE IT SLOW AND DON'T COMPLAIN
MY POOR HEART JUST CAN'T STAND THE STRAIN
HEY, I CAN CURE YOUR DISEASE
LET'S HEAR YOU SAY PRETTY PLEASE
AND TAKE YOUR MEDICINE DOWN ON YOUR KNEES!

DANNY.
OH, BABY, TAKE MY RING 'CAUSE YOU'RE MY MATCH
SANDY.
WELL, I STILL THINK THERE'S STRINGS ATTACHED
DANNY.
YOU'RE WRITIN' MY EPITAPH
SANDY.
WELL THAT'S JUST TOUGH AND A HALF
DANNY.
YOU'RE GONNA MAKE ME DIE!
SANDY.
DON'T MAKE ME LAUGH!

DANNY and SANDY.
WELL, I MIGHT FORGIVE WHAT YOU PUT ME THROUGH
CAUSE I DO BELIEVE YOU REALLY LOVE ME TOO
I LOOK IN YOUR EYES
THE SUFFERING DIES
UH-HUH! I'M ALL CHOKED UP
ALL KIDS.
HEY, HEY, HEY, YEAH
I'M ALL CHOKED UP
DANNY and SANDY.
HEY, HEY, HEY, YEAH
I'M ALL CHOKED UP

EVERYBODY.
HEY, HEY, HEY, YEAH
I'M-ALL-CHOKED-UP!!!!!!!!!!!!!!!!! OW!

DANNY. Hey, Sandy, I still got my ring! I guess you're still kinda mad at me, huh?
SANDY. Nah. Forget about it! Gimme that thing!

(They hug quickly.)

ROGER. Hey, we just gonna stand around here all day? Let's get outta here!
DOODY. Yeah, we're missin' "Anything Can Happen" Day!
SONNY. Hey, Marty, did I tell ya I'm gettin' a new Impala?
MARTY. Ohh, would you paint my name on it?

(SONNY nods "sure." He puts his arm around her.) I feel like *(whispers to Kenickie)* celebrating!
RIZZO. ~~Hey, Kenickie, can we stop by the Dairy Queen? How's about a little party?~~ Black Cows all around. My treat!
SANDY. Hey, Patty, you wanna come?
PATTY. Well, thanks, but I wouldn't want to be in the way. Plus, I don't really have a date.
DANNY. Hey, I know just the guy. Right you guys!
ALL. Hey, Eugene!
EUGENE. *(Entering in black leather motorcycle jacket with his hair in a greased-up pompadour.)* A-wop-ba-ba-lu-bop!
ALL. A Wop-Bam-Boom!

(The kids all have their arms around each other as they sing a reprise of "We Go Together" and then go off dancing and singing.)

CURTAIN

PROPERTY PLOT

<u>PRESET ON STAGE</u>

D.C. cafeteria table covered with white tablecloth (pennants and sign
    facing D.S.)
Rostrum on top of table with three green yearbooks on either side
Small business card left of rostrum
Long green bench U.S. of table with mic clips facing U.S.
U.L. corner of S.R. steps:
    Spiral notebook
    Textbook
    Comic book
    1 bottle of Coke
    2 slices of bread (to look like a sandwich) in wax paper bag (in
        brown paper bag
D.R. corner of S.R. steps (on lowest step):
    Brown paper bag with orange
    Water pistol
    Binder
    Textbook
2 cafeteria chairs on stage side of S.L. tab

On Sandy's bed (on upper deck):
    Spread
    Pillow
    Throw pillow
    Box of Kleenex
    6 stuffed animals (at headboard)
    Microphone (practical—tucked under pillow)
On end table:
    Lamp
    Radio
On top shelf:
    Telephone
On bottom shelf:
    2 stuffed animals

<u>PRESET OFF RIGHT</u>

For Act I, Scene 1 (Alma Mater and Parody):
    Guitar

For Act I, Scene 2 (Cafeteria):
    Brown paper bag with pink "Hostess Snowball"
    Binder
    Textbook
For Act I, Scene 3 (Magic Changes):
    Textbook
    Guitar chord book (Ronnie Dell)
For Act I, Scene 5 (Hubcap):
    4 hubcaps
    1 pair of red foam dice on red string
    Tire iron
    Car ("Greased Lightning") with box of Saran Wrap in front
    Police siren and air horn
For Act I, Scene 6 (Baton):
    4 2-inch strips of white adhesive tape
For Act I, Scene 7 (Park):
    Picnic table with the following on top:
        6-pack of Coke (small green glass bottles—not practical)
        6 Coke bottles (2 with drinkable water—marked with tape)
        3 hamburger rolls in wax paper bags
        Church key

For Act II, Scene 2 (Track and Rumble):
    Hair-do magazine
    Track relay baton
    Automobile antenna
For Act II, Scene 4 (Basement):
    Bar unit with 2 stools and the following on top:
        Bowl of potato chips
        Small bag of popcorn
        6 Coke bottles (small green glass type; 2 with drinkable
            water—marked with tape)
        6-pack of Coke (not practical)
        "View-Master" with slide
        45 rpm turntable with 4 records
        Sofa with the following on top:
            Large throw pillow
            Guitar
        Canvas butterfly chair

PRESENT OFF LEFT

For Act I, Scene 1 (Alma Mater and Parody):
    Black purse (Patty)
For Act I, Scene 2 (Cafeteria):
    5 tray set-ups on prop table:
        1: Marty
            Cafeteria tray
            Knife, fork and spoon
            Large plate (rice pudding)
            Large bowl (fruit salad)
            Small bowl (rice pudding)
            Plastic "glass" (interior painted purple for grape;
                attached to tray with Velcro)
            Napkin
            Bubble gum
            Black looseleaf binder
            Magazine
            Purse containing comb and glasses
        2. Jan
            Cafeteria tray
            Fork and spoon
            Large plate (rice pudding)
            2 small bowls (rice pudding and fruit salad)
            Large bowl (fruit salad)
            Plastic "glass"—(interior painted white for milk; can be
                glued to tray)
            Banana
            Napkin
            Bubble gum
            Looseleaf binder
            Textbook
            Purse containing datebook
        3. Sandy
            Cafeteria tray
            Knife and fork
            Large plate
            Small bowl (rice pudding)
            Plastic glass (interior painted white; can be glued to tray)
            Napkin
            Looseleaf binder

Term paper binder
Textbook
Purse containing comb
4. Frenchy
    Cafeteria tray
    Fork and spoon
    Large plate (fruit salad)
    Plastic "glass" (interior purple; can be glued to tray)
    Napkin
    Bubble gum
    Large black looseleaf binder
    2 movie star magazines
    Green purse containing makeup stick and emery board
5. Rizzo
    Cafeteria tray
    Large plate (fruit salad)
    Knife, fork and spoon
    Large bowl (fruit salad)
    Small bowl (fruit salad)
    Plastic "glass" (interior purple; can be glued to tray)
    Bubble gum
    Napkin
    Black purse with long arm strap
Pack of 6 small colored cards
Class schedule
Purse
Black binder
Brown paper bag containing 2 apples
For Act I, Scene 3 (Magic Changes):
2 green pom poms
Book
Eraser
For Act I, Scene 4 (Pajama Party):
Bed with headboard
Black "Pink Lady" jacket (on bed)
Circle pin (pinned on jacket)
Bedside table
Make-up mirror (soaped) on stand (on bedside table)
Red nail polish (in bedside table drawer)
On shelf below:
    Stuffed animal

Hat box

Kleenex

2 books

Vanity table

Wallet surrounded by three rubber bands and containing
long series of pictures, a marked picture removable (in table
drawer)

Open magazine (on table)

Foot stool (under table)

Chair

Blanket with the following on top:

Portable radio

Twinkies

Comic book

For Act I, Scene 6 (Baton):

2 batons

For Act I, Scene 7 (Park):

2 45-degree-angle park benches (one stacked upside down on top
of the other)

Battered trash can

Blanket

3 magazines

2 bags of leaves

For Act II, Scene 1 (Hop):

Red "Johnny Casino" guitar (not practical)

For Act II, Scene 2 (Track, B.S.D., Rumble):

Lead pipe

Chain

Baseball bat

Zip gun (covered with rubber band)

White rolled "diploma" tied with red ribbon

For Act II, Scene 3 (Drive-In):

Car with Sandy's purse on front seat

For Act II, Scene 5 (Burger):

Burger booth unit

Burger counter and stool unit

Menu (on top of counter)

Bucket containing Coke bottle with coke (inside counter)

ACT II PRESET ON STAGE

Hot table (U.C. between columns) with the following on top:
    Green tablecloth with "coconuts" and green crepe streamers
    Punch bowl
    Ladle
    8 cups
    Card of tacks
    Pink crepe streamer
Long green bench (D.C. on marks)
Tray of prizes (Upper deck D.L. corner of bedroom platform):
    2 record albums ("Hits from The House of Wax")
    2 3 x 5 cards (movie passes)
    1 2 x 3 card (gift certificate)
    2 trophies

STAGE LEFT RUNNING PLOT

During Act I, Scene 1 (Parody):
    Catch black purse from girl (Patty)
    Set in first section of prop table
During Act I, Scene 2 (Cafeteria):
    Fold tablecloth and store
    Store green yearbooks
During Act II, Scene 2 (Magic Changes):
    Clear cafeteria table
    Place dishes in strainer
    Store table U.S.
    Wipe off trays and reset on prop table
During Act I, Scene 4 (Pajama Party):
    Set following on prop table:
        Blanket
        2 magazines
        Black handbag (Rizzo)
During Act I, Scene 5 (Hubcap):
    Catch bed, dresser and chair
    Replace picture in wallet
    Set green tablecloth
    Set punchbowl with ladle and paper cups (2 stacks of 4 each)
    Set roll of crepe streamers and thumbtacks on dresser
    Set circle pin on Pink Lady jacket

During Act I, Scene 6 (Baton):
>   Car comes off
>   Clear and take S.R. Saran wrap, hubcaps and dice
>   Preset Sandy's purse in front seat of car
>   Preset park benches to go on

During Intermission:
>   Strike trash can, books from lockers, pom poms from upper deck

Preset for Act II:
>   Prizes on tray D.L. corner of bedroom platform (on upper deck):
>>   2 trophies
>>   2 record albums
>>   2 3 x 5 cards
>>   1 3x 2 card
>   Long green bench D.L. on marks
>   Hop table U.C. between columns
>   Book in fourth locker from center on bottom
>   Coke bottle (with Coke) in bucket in burger counter unit
>   Books and dishes on trays (prop table)

During Act II, Scene 2 (Track):
>   Take red guitar from actor on upper deck (Casino) and hang it on
>   prop shelf
>   Take hop table from actresses (Lynch and Patty)
>   Clear and store cloth, etc.
>   Store dresser with other bedroom pieces
>   Take green bench from actor (Eugene) and store U.S.

During Act II, Scene 3 (Drive-In):
>   Store lead pipe and chain, baseball bat and zip gun
>   Take aerial S.R.

During Act II, Scene 4 (Basement):
>   Set burger units (booth and counter) in position to go on

During Act II, Scene 5 (Burger):
>   Catch burger counter unit from actor (Eugene) and store

STAGE RIGHT RUNNING PLOT

During Act I, Scene 2 (Cafeteria):
>   Take green yearbooks from lady (Lynch)
>   Take scrim leg from man (Kenickie) and store U.S.

During Act I, Scene II (Hubcap):
>   As car goes on, move picnic table down to same preset position
>   car was in

During intermission:
    Clear mics from picnic table and strike picnic table
    Preset on bar unit with two stools:
        6-pack of Coke
        6 Coke bottles (2 with drinkable water—marked with tape)
        1 small bag of popcorn
        1 bowl of potato chips
    Preset bar unit in position originally used by car D.S. of bar
    Preset sofa with large throw pillow and butterfly chair

During Act II, Scene 5 (Burger):
    Catch bar unit, sofa and butterfly chair with large throw pillow
        and store
    Strike two green pom poms
    Catch burger booth unit and store

RUNNING PLOT

During Act I, Scene 2 (Cafeteria):
    Take green yearbooks from S.R. and tablecloth from U.C. to S.L.
    Fold cloth and store
    Store yearbooks
During Act I, Scene 3 (Major Changes):
    Clear cafeteria table
    Set trays and books on prop table
During Act I, Scene 4 (Pajama Party):
    Store cafeteria chairs U.S.
During Act I, Scene 5 (Greased Lightning):
    Catch bed and chair
    Store blanket with comic book wrapped in it
During Act I, Scene 6 (Baton):
    Position park benches to go on
    Wash dishes

During Intermission:
    Strike blanket S.L.
    Strike magazines S.L.
    Strike benches S.L.
    Take leaf bag from S.R. to S.L.

During Act II, Scene 2 (Track):
    Take prizes from R. and store S.L.

COSTUME PLOT

DANNY ZUKO

Act I

Scenes 2 & 3: Black stretch pants with pink stitching on sides, white
t-shirt, black leather jacket, belt, white socks, blue suede shoes,
medal and chain

Scene 5: Same minus black leather jacket

Scene 6: Add purple short-sleeved shirt with white trim (unbuttoned)

Scene 7: Same as Act I, Scene 2

Act II

Scene 1: Black stretch slacks, red socks, blue suede shoes, black
tricot see-thru shirt, red sport jacket with silver lining

Scene 2: White track suit (green trimmed shorts and tank top), white
socks, white basketball sneakers, neck chain and medal

Scene 3: Purple pullover shirt with gray piping, black stretch slacks,
white socks, blue suede shoes, neck chain and medal

Scene 5: Black stretch slacks, sleeveless t-shirt, black leather jacket,
neck chain and medal, white socks, blue suede shoes

SANDY DUMBROWKSI

Act I

Scene 2: Pink and white striped shirt blouse, gray felt circle skirt with
pink poodle trim, cinch belt (clear plastic if possible), white
socks, brown loafers, blue hair ribbon

Scene 4: Floor-length, baby blue bathrobe with small floral print,
fluffy fur slippers, blue ribbon

Scene 6: Gym suit (should be "Rydell green" with name lettered on in
white), white socks, white sneakers, blue hair ribbon, white
adhesive tape under left earlobe

Scene 7: Same as Scene 2; change to white cinch belt, black Capezios,
white ribbon

Act II

Scene 1: Same as Act I, Scene 4

Scene 2: White slip, white slippers, white on white striped plastic
shower curtain cape, white hairnet, white roller headpiece

Scene 3: Pale blue straight skirt, white ruffled nylon blouse, hair
ribbon. blue heels

Scene 4: Blue and gray plaid tight skirt, white "angora" bead-trimmed sweater, black Capezios, hair ribbon

Scene 5: Chartreuse-y green pedal pushers, black leotard top, black cinch belt, black leather jacket studded on back to say "Big D," black Capezios, flashy earrings

MISS LYNCH

Act I

Scenes 1 & 2: Black full slip, black and white flower print dress, black pumps, pearl necklace.

Act II

Scene 1: Add flower corsage, pearl necklace
Curtain: Same as Act I, Scene 1

PATTY SIMCOX

Act I

Scene 1: Black skirt, gray jacket, black and white scarf, black shoes, black shoulder purse, gold earrings

Scenes 2 & 6: Green and brown pleated cheerleader skirt, cheerleader sweater, green and brown hair ribbon, white socks, white sneakers, "Vote Patty" cardboard campaign pin on sweater

Act II

Scene 1: Pink prom dress with crinolines, pink heels, wrist corsage
Scene 2: White slip, white slippers, white on white striped plastic shower curtain cape, white hairnet, white roller headpiece
Scene 5: Same as Act I, Scene 2

EUGENE FLORCZYK

ACT I

Scene 1: Gray suit, white shirt, red tie, black shoes
Scene 7: Camel Boy Scout Bermudas, white shirt, green sweater, yellow and brown argyle socks, brown loafers

ACT II

Scene 1: White formal shirt, cufflinks and studs, black 50's tuxedo, white buck shoes, gray and black argyle socks, yellow plaid bow tie and cummerbund
Curtain: Same as Act I, Scene 1

JAN

Act I

Scenes 2 & 3: Plaid pleated skirt, red short-sleeved sweater with white
angora trim at top, yellow scarf, white socks, black Capezios

Scene 4: Bright yellow print shortie pajama top and panties, white
socks

Scene 7: Red sweater, flower print pedal pushers, yellow scarf, Pink
Lady jacket, white socks, black Capezios

Act II

Scene 1: Blue brocade prom dress, white Capezios, rhinestone
headband, white crinoline

Scene 2: White slip, white slippers, white on white striped plastic
shower curtain cape, white hairnet, white roller headpiece

Scene 4: Same as Act I, Scene 2

Scene 5: Flower print pedal pushers, red sweater, yellow scarf on
head, white socks, black Capezios, Pink Lady jacket

MARTY

Act I

Scenes 2 & 3: Black straight skirt, sky blue cardigan sweater, pink
and blue scarf, Pink Lady jacket, white socks, black Capezios,
flashy earrings, pink eye frames with rhinestones

Scene 4: Pink pajama top and panties, gold short-heel slippers, pink
headband, gold earrings, short red Japanese kimono

Scene 7: Black skirt, sky blue sweater, black Capezios, blue and white
scarf, blue hair band, white letter sweater with H.C.

Act II

Scene 1: Gold beaded sweater, tight gold skirt, gold heels, big
earrings, headband

Scene 2: White slip, white slippers, white on white striped plastic
shower curtain cape, white hairnet, white roller headpiece

Scene 4: Black skirt, sky blue sweater, blue and white scarf, purple
headband, black Capezios, Pink Lady jacket worn around waist

Scene 5: Same as Act I, Scene 2

BETTY RIZZO

Act I

Scenes 1 & 2: Tight blue straight skirt, turquoise blue fuzzy (angora type) long-sleeve sweater, Pink Lady jacket, red Capezios, anklets. *Underdress:* pajama bottoms, red and white striped pullover jersey)

Scene 4: Blue or green pajama top and panties, red Capezios. *Underdress:* red and white striped top; *Preset* white pedal pushers

Scene 5: White pedal pushers, red and white striped top, black cinch belt, red Capezios

Scene 7: Add Pink Lady jacket

Act II

Scene 1: Black prom dress, black heels

Scene 2: White slip, white slippers, white on white striped plastic shower curtain cape, white hairnet, white roller headpiece

Scene 4: White pedal pushers, turquoise fuzzy sweater, red Capezios

Scene 5: Add Pink Lady jacket

DOODY

Act I

Scenes 2 & 3: Blue jeans, white t-shirt, red plaid flannel shirt, white socks, black belt, brown penny loafers

Scene 5: Blue jeans, white t-shirt with v-neck, white socks, brown loafers

Scene 7: Same as Act 1, Scene 2

Act II

Scene 1: Black cuffed slacks, pink and black shirt, white sport coat, white socks, brown loafers

Scene 2: Blue jeans, red, blue and white pullover, windbreaker-type shirt, white socks, loafers

Scenes 4 & 5: Same as Act I, Scene 2

ROGER

Act I

Scenes 2 & 3: Gray slacks with pink stitching on sides, white t-shirt, burgundy windbreaker, white socks, engineer boots

Scene 5: Gray pants, white t-shirt, white socks, engineer boots

Scene 7: Add Hawaiian flowered shirt (unbuttoned), brown loafers

Act II

Scene 1: Gray slacks, yellow plaid shirt, pink sport jacket, white socks, brown loafers

Scene 2: Blue jeans with special Velcro, white t-shirt, burgundy
    windbreaker, white socks, brown loafers.
Scene 4: Gray slacks, yellow plaid shirt, white socks, brown loafers
Scene 5: Same as Act I, Scene 2

KENICKIE

Act I

Scenes 2, 3, 5 & 7: Blue jeans, black t-shirt, silver belt, black leather
    jacket

Act II

Scene 1: Gray slacks, black embroidered cowboy shirt, bola tie,
    madras sport jacket, black socks, boots, red bandana handkerchief
    in right pants pocket
Scene 2: Gray slacks, black t-shirt, gray belt, black leather jacket,
    black socks, boots
Scene 4: Blue jeans, black cowboy shirt, black socks, boots
Scene 5: Same as Act I, Scene 2

SONNY LaTIERRI

Act I

Scenes 2 & 3: Black slacks, white t-shirt, chain and medal, tan leather
    jacket, white socks, black pointed shoes, small black brim hat,
    dark glasses, black belt
Scene 5: Black pants, white socks, black pointed shoes, black belt,
    white tank top undershirt, black brim hat
Scene 7: Remove black hat and add tan leather jacket

Act II

Scene 1: Black slacks, black shirt, white tie, shiny green sport coat,
    white socks, black pointed shoes
Scene 2: Same as Act I, Scene 2 minus dark glasses
Scene 4: Same as Act I, Scene 2 minus dark glasses, black hat and tan
    leather jacket
Scene 5: Same as Act I, Scene 2 minus hat and dark glasses

FRENCHY

Act I

Scenes 2 & 3: Gray tweed straight skirt with godets, hot pink sweater,
    pink scarf, Pink Lady jacket, white socks, black Capezios, flashy

earrings
Scene 4: Lavender shortie pajama top and panties, white socks
Scene 7: Same as Act I, Scene 2

Act II

Scenes 1: Nylon green blouse, black velvet diagonally-striped skirt,
    green high heels (pointy-toed spikes), flashy earrings
Scene 2: Same as Act I, Scene 2
Scene 4: Remove Pink Lady jacket
Scene 5: Same as Act I, Scene 2

VINCE FONTAINE

Act II

Scene 1 and Curtain: Black tuxedo slacks, gold dress shirt, cufflinks
    and studs, black cummerbund, black bow tie, leopard tuxedo
    jacket, black socks, black patent leather shoes

JOHNNY CASINO

Act II

Scene 1: Geranium pink slacks with dark stripes on side, pink ruffed
    formal shirt, large cufflinks, red bow tie, pink plaid tuxedo jacket
    with red lapels, white socks, pink and red two-toned wing-tipped
    shoes, red cummerbund

CHA-CHA DeGREGORIO

Act II

Scene 1: Yellow taffeta prom dress with crinolines, yellow tyette
    shoes, yellow hair ribbon, yellow and green poppet bead necklace
Scene 2: White slip, white slippers, white on white striped plastic
    shower curtain cape, white hairnet, white roller headpiece
Curtain: Same as Act 2, Scene 1

TEEN ANGEL

Act II

Scene 2 and Curtain: White sweater, white slacks, white socks, white
    bucks

COSTUMES: RUNNING ORDER

Act I, Scene 1

MISS LYNCH: Black full slip, black and white flower dress print, black pumps. pearl necklace

EUGENE: Gray suit, white shirt, red tie, black shoes

PATTY: Black skirt, gray jacket, black and white scarf, black shoes, black shoulder purse, gold earrings.

Act I, Scene 2

DANNY: Black stretch pants with pink stitching on sides, white t-shirt, black leather jacket, belt, white socks, blue suede shoes, medal and chain

KENICKIE: Blue jeans, black t-shirt, silver belt, black leather jacket, black socks, boots

ROGER: Gray slacks with pink stitching on sides, white t-shirt, burgundy windbreaker, white socks, engineer boots

SONNY: Black slacks, white t-shirt, black shirt, chain and medal, tan leather jacket, white socks, black pointed shoes, small black brim hat, dark glasses, black belt

DOODY: Blue jeans, white t-shirt, red plaid flannel shirt, white socks, black belt, brown penny loafers

RIZZO: Tight blue straight skirt, turquoise blue fuzzy (angora-type) long- sleeve sweater, Pink Lady jacket, red Capezios, anklet
Underdress: Pajama bottoms, red and white striped pullover jersey

FRENCHY: Gray tweed straight skirt with godets, hot pink sweater, pink scarf, Pink Lady jacket, white socks, black Capezios, flashy earrings

JAN: Plaid pleated skirt, red short-sleeved sweater with white angora trim at top, yellow scarf, white socks, black Capezios

MARTY: Black straight skirt, sky blue cardigan sweater, pink and blue scarf, Pink Lady jacket, pink hair band, earrings, black Capezios, pink eye frames with rhinestones

SANDY: Pink and white striped shirt blouse, gray felt circle skirt with pink poodle trim, cinch belt (clear plastic if possible), white socks, brown loafers, blue hair ribbon

PATTY: Green and brown pleated cheerleader skirt, cheerleader sweater, green and brown hair ribbon, white socks, white sneakers, "Vote Patty" cardboard pin on sweater

MISS LYNCH: same as Act I, Scene 1

Act I, Scene 3
Same as Act I, Scene 2

Act I, Scene 4
(All pajamas are shorties)
FRENCHY: Lavender pajama top and panties, white socks
JAN: Bright yellow print pajama top and panties, white socks
RIZZO: Blue or green pajama top and panties, red Capezios.
 Underdress: red and white striped top; _Preset_ white pedal
 pushers)
MARTY: Pink pajama top and panties, gold short-heel slipper, pink
 headband, gold earrings, short Japanese kimono
SANDY: Floor-length baby blue bathrobe with small floral print,
 fluffy fur slippers, blue ribbon

Act I, Scene 5
DANNY: Same as Act I, Scene 2 minus the black leather jacket
SONNY: Same as Act I, Scene 2 minus white t-shirt, dark glasses,
 black shirt, tan leather jacket; add tank top undershirt
ROGER: Gray pants, white t-shirt, white socks, engineer boots
DOODY: Blue jeans, white t-shirt with v-neck, white socks, brown
 loafers
RIZZO: White pedal pushers, red and white striped top, black cinch
 belt, red Capezios
KENICKIE: Same as Act I, Scene 2

Act I, Scene 6
SANDY: Gym suit (should be "Rydell green" with name lettered on
 in white), white socks, white sneakers, blue hair ribbon, white
 adhesive tape under left earlobe
PATTY Same as Act I, Scene 2
DANNY: Add white short-sleeved shirt with purple trim (unbuttoned

Act I, Scene 7
ROGER: Add Hawaiian flowered shirt (unbuttoned), brown loafers
JAN: Red sweater, flower print pedal pushers, yellow scarf, Pink
 Lady jacket, white socks, black Capezios
DANNY: Same as Act I, Scene 2
MARTY: Black skirt, sky blue sweater, black Capezios, blue and
 white scarf, blue hair band, white letter sweater with "H.C."
RIZZO. Add Pink Lady jacket

KENICKIE: Same as Act I, Scenes 2 and 5

EUGENE: Camel Boy Scout Bermudas, white shirt, green sweater, yellow and brown argyle socks, brown loafers

SANDY: Same as Act I, Scene 2; change to white cinch belt, black Capezios, white hair ribbon

DOODY: Same as Act One, Scene 2

FRENCHY: Same as Act I, Scene 2

SONNY: Same as Act I, Scene 5 minus black hat; add tan leather jacket

Act II, Scene 1

DANNY: Black stretch slacks, red socks, blue suede shoes, black tricot see-thru shirt, red sport jacket with silver lining

RIZZO: Black prom dress, black heels

FRENCHY: Nylon green blouse, black velvet diagonally striped skirt, green high heels (pointy-toed spikes), flashy earrings

JAN: Blue brocade prom dress, white Capezios, rhinestone headband, white crinoline

MARTY: Gold beaded sweater, tight gold skirt, gold heels, big earrings, headband

KENICKIE: Gray slacks, black embroidered cowboy shirt, bola tie, madras sport jacket, black socks, boots, red bandana handkerchief in right pants pocket

SONNY: Black slacks, black shirt, white tie, shiny green sport coat, white socks, black pointed shoes

ROGER: Gray slacks, yellow plaid shirt, pink sport jacket, white socks, brown loafers

DOODY: Black cuffed slacks, pint and black shirt, white sport coat, white socks, brown loafers

EUGENE: White formal shirt, cuff links and studs, black 50's tuxedo, white buck shoes, gray and black argyle socks, yellow plaid bow tie and cummerbund

MISS LYNCH: Same as Act I, Scene 1; add flower corsage, pearl necklace

PATTY: Pink prom dress, pink heels, wrist corsage (dress with crinolines)

JOHNNY CASINO: Geranium pink slacks with dark stripes on side, pink ruffed formal shirt, large cufflinks, red bow tie, pink plaid tuxedo jacket with red lapels, white socks, pink and red two-toned wing-tipped shoes, red cummerbund

VINCE FONTAINE: Black tuxedo slacks, gold dress shirt, cufflinks

and studs, black cummerbund, black bow tie, leopard tuxedo
jacket, black socks, black patent leather shoes

CHA-CHA DeGREGORIO: Yellow taffeta prom dress with
crinolines, yellow tyette shoes, yellow hair ribbon, yellow and
green poppet bead necklace

SANDY: Same as Act I, Scene 4

Act II, Scene 2

KENICKIE: Gray slacks, black t-shirt, gray belt, black leather jacket,
black socks, boots

SONNY: Same as Act I, Scene 2 minus dark glasses

DOODY: Blue jeans, red, blue and white pullover windbreaker-type
shirt, white socks, loafers

FRENCHY: Same as Act I, Scene 2

GIRLS: White slips, white slippers, white on white striped plastic
shower curtain capes, white hairnets, white roller headpieces

TEEN ANGEL: White sweater, white slacks, white socks, white
bucks

DANNY: White track suit (green trimmed shorts and tank top), white
socks, white basketball sneakers, neck chain and medal

ROGER: Blue jeans with special Velcro, white t-shirt burgundy
windbreaker, white socks, brown loafers

Act II, Scene 3

DANNY: Purple pullover shirt with gray piping, black stretch slacks,
white socks, blue suede shoes, neck chain and medal

SANDY: Pale blue straight skirt, white ruffled nylon blouse, hair
ribbon, blue heels

Act II, Scene 4

SANDY: Blue and gray plaid tight skirt, white "angora" bead-
trimmed sweater, black Capezios, hair ribbon

RIZZO: White pedal pushers, turquoise fuzzy sweater, red Capezios

MARTY: Black skirt, sky blue sweater, blue and white scarf, purple
headband, black Capezios, Pink Lady jacket worn around waist

FRENCHY: Same as Act I, Scene 2 minus Pink Lady jacket

JAN: Same as Act 1, Scene 2

KENICKIE: Blue jeans, black cowboy shirt, black socks, boots

ROGER: Gray slacks, yellow plaid shirt, white socks, brown loafers

SONNY: Same as Act 1, Scene 2 minus dark glasses, black hat and
tan leather jacket

Act II, Scene 5
ROGER: Same as Act I, Scene 2
SONNY: Same as Act I, Scene 2 minus hat and dark glasses
KENICKIE: Same as Act I, Scene 2
DOODY: Same as Act I, Scene 2
PATTY: Same as Act 1, Scene 2
DANNY: Black stretch slacks, black sleeveless t-shirt, black leather
    jacket, neck chain and medal, white socks, blue suede shoes
RIZZO: White pedal pushers, turquoise fuzzy sweater, red Capezios,
    Pink Lady jacket
JAN: Flower print pedal pushers, red sweater, yellow scarf on head,
    white socks, black Capezios, Pink Lady jacket
FRENCHY: Same as Act I, Scene 2
MARTY: Same as Act 1, Scene 2
SANDY: Chartreuse-y green pedal pushers, black leotard top, black
    cinch belt, black leather jacket studded on back to say "Big D,"
    black Capezios, flashy earrings

Curtain Calls
CHA-CHA: Same as Act II, Scene 1
TEEN ANGEL: Same as Act II, Scene 2
VINCE FONTAINE: Same as Act II, Scene 1
MISS LYNCH: Same as Act I, Scene 1
EUGENE: Same as Act I, Scene 1

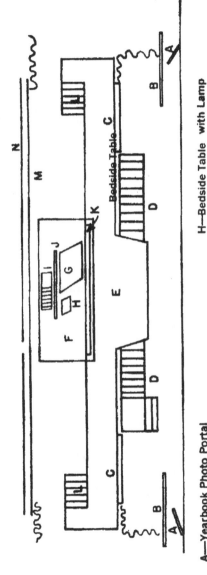

A—Yearbook Photo Portal
B—#1 Greaser Wings
C—#2 Greaser Wings
D—Moving School Stairs
E—Elevated Platform
F—Sandy's Bedroom (Elevated)
G—Sandy's Bed

H—Bedside Table with Lamp
I—Escape Stairs
J—Sandra Dee Blow-up Photo
K—James Dean Photo
L—Escape Stairs
M—Photo Collage Drop
N—Brick Wall Drop

FLOOR PLAN
"GREASE"

ALSO AVAILABLE FROM SAMUEL FRENCH

SECRET GARDEN
The Musical

Book and Lyrics by Marsha Norman
Music by Lucy Simon
Based on the novel by Frances Hodgson Burnett

12m, 10f, 1f child, (doubling possible) / Ints., exts.

This enchanting classic of children's literature is now a brilliant musical by a Pulitzer Prize winning playwright. Orphaned in India, an 11 year old girl returns to Yorkshire to live with an embittered, reclusive uncle and his invalid son. The estate includes a magic locked garden. Flashbacks, dream sequences, a strolling chorus of ghosts, and some of the most beautiful music ever written for Broadway dramatize *The Secret Garden*'s compelling tale of regeneration. This Tony Award winner is a treasure for children and adults.

"Elegant, entrancing.... The best American musical of the Broadway season."
– *Time*

"A splendid, intelligent musical...It's all you can hope for in children's theatre. But the best surprise is that this show is the most adult new musical of the season."
– *U.S.A. Today*

"Revels in theatrical imagination [and] achieves the irresistible appeal that moves audiences to standing ovations."
– *Christian Science Monitor*

SAMUELFRENCH.COM

ALSO AVAILABLE FROM SAMUEL FRENCH

THE WIZ
The New Musical Version of *The Wonderful Wizard of Oz*
by L. Frank Baum

Book by William F. Brown
Music and Lyrics by Charlie Smalls

11 principals, extras / Various sets

Dorothy's adventures in the Land of Oz have been set to music in a dazzling, lively mixture of rock, gospel and soul music. Everybody knows the story, but now it's a new fantasy for today– mysterious, opulent and fanciful.

"Radiates so much energy you can hardly sit in your seat... great fun."
– *New York Post*

"A continuous festival of movement...splendid character songs."
– *Women's Wear Daily*

"A carnival of fun...wickedly amusing show."
– *Time*

"A virtual musical circus...driving rhythms, soaring songs... boisterous, exuberant."
– WABC TV

SAMUEL FRENCH STAFF

Nate Collins
President

Ken Dingledine
Director of Operations,
Vice President

Bruce Lazarus
Executive Director

Rita Maté
Director of Finance

ACCOUNTING

Lori Thimsen | Director of Licensing Compliance
Nehal Kumar | Senior Accounting Associate
Josephine Messina | Accounts Payable
Helena Mezzina | Royalty Administration
Joe Garner | Royalty Administration
Jessica Zheng | Accounts Receivable
Andy Lian | Accounts Receivable
Zoe Qiu | Accounts Receivable
Charlie Sou | Accounting Associate
Joann Mannello | Orders Administrator

BUSINESS AFFAIRS

Lysna Marzani | Director of Business Affairs
Kathryn McCumber | Business Administrator

CUSTOMER SERVICE AND LICENSING

Brad Lohrenz | Director of Licensing Development
Billie Davis | Licensing Service Manager
Fred Schnitzer | Business Development Manager
Melody Fernandez | Amateur Licensing Supervisor
Laura Lindson | Professional Licensing Supervisor
John Tracey | Professional Licensing Associate
Kim Rogers | Amateur Licensing Associate
Matthew Akers | Amateur Licensing Associate
Jay Clark | Amateur Licensing Associate
Alicia Grey | Amateur Licensing Associate
Ashley Byrne | Amateur Licensing Associate
Jake Glickman | Amateur Licensing Associate
Chris Lonstrup | Amateur Licensing Associate
Jabez Zuniga | Amateur Licensing Associate
Glenn Halcomb | Amateur Licensing Associate
Derek Hassler | Amateur Licensing Associate
Jennifer Carter | Amateur Licensing Associate

EDITORIAL AND PUBLICATIONS

Amy Rose Marsh | Literary Manager
Ben Coleman | Editorial Associate
Gene Sweeney | Graphic Designer
David Geer | Publications Supervisor
Charlyn Brea | Publications Associate
Tyler Mullen | Publications Associate

MARKETING

Abbie Van Nostrand | Director of Marketing
Alison Sundstrom | Marketing Associate

OPERATIONS

Joe Ferreira | Product Development Manager
Casey McLain | Operations Supervisor
Danielle Heckman | Office Coordinator, Reception

SAMUEL FRENCH BOOKSHOP (LOS ANGELES)

Joyce Mehess | Bookstore Manager
Cory DeLair | Bookstore Buyer
Jennifer Palumbo | Customer Service Associate
Sonya Wallace | Bookstore Associate
Tim Coultas | Bookstore Associate
Monté Patterson | Bookstore Associate
Robin Hushbeck | Bookstore Associate
Alfred Contreras | Shipping & Receiving

LONDON OFFICE

Felicity Barks | Submissions Associate
Steve Blacker | Bookshop Associate
David Bray | Customer Services Associate
Zena Choi | Professional Licensing Associate
Robert Cooke | Assistant Buyer
Stephanie Dawson | Amateur Licensing Associate
Simon Ellison | Retail Sales Manager
Jason Felix | Royalty Administration
Susan Griffiths | Amateur Licensing Associate
Robert Hamilton | Amateur Licensing Associate
Lucy Hume | Publications Associate
Nasir Khan | Management Accountant
Simon Magniti | Royalty Administration
Louise Mappley | Amateur Licensing Associate
James Nicolau | Despatch Associate
Martin Phillips | Librarian
Zubayed Rahman | Despatch Associate
Steve sanderson | Royalty Administration Supervisor
Roger Sheppard | I.T. Manager
Geoffrey Skinner | Company Accountant
Peter Smith | Amateur Licensing Associate
Garry Spratley | Customer Service Manager
David Webster | UK Operations Director

SAMUELFRENCH.COM
SAMUELFRENCH-LONDON.CO.UK

Get the name of your cast and crew in print with Special Editions!

Special Editions are a unique, fun way to commemorate your production and RAISE MONEY.

The Samuel French Special Edition is a customized script personalized to *your* production. Your cast and crew list, photos from your production and special thanks will all appear in a Samuel French Acting Edition alongside the original text of the play.

These Special Editions are powerful fundraising tools that can be sold in your lobby or throughout your community in advance.

These books have autograph pages that make them perfect for year book memories, or gifts for relatives unable to attend the show. Family and friends will cherish this one of a kind souvenier.

Everyone will want a copy of these beautiful, personalized scripts!

Order Your copies today!
E-MAIL SPECIALEDITIONS@SAMUELFRENCH.COM
OR CALL US AT 1-866-598-8449!